Ep. 01:
Black Water

InkRose

Anastasia Snyder

InkRoseInc.com

Cover text layout by Karen Y. Snyder
Cover illustration by Anastasia Snyder
Ink Rose ™ logo designed by Karen Y. Snyder
Copy Editing by Fred Johnson

ISBN 978-0-9985828-2-5 (ePub eBook)
ISBN 978-0-9985828-3-2 (Black and White Print)
ISBN 978-0-9985828-4-9 (Color Print)

Dedication

Alright folks, let me slap down some 'thank yous' to the people who helped me make this thing happen.

First off to my family, who have always been supportive of my artistic endeavors.

Second off, to the friends I've met both on-line and off, both on Discord and in the real world. They read through the first drafts and helped to encouraged me through the writing process.

Third, to my editor, Fred Johnson. He gave a lot of great feedback and suggestions that overall led to a much better final product.

Fourth, to a bunch of YouTubers whos sensuous voices kept me entertained while drawing a lot of these illustrations. Thanks, Pewds. Also thanks to those long music compilation videos that got me in the mood for writing.

Last but not least, thanks to the big G-boy in heaven. Nice job making me, my dude.

Series Order

-Book 1-

Spectral Lakes: Black Water

-Book 2-

Spectral Lakes: Wolf Skin

(Coming Soon)

Chapters

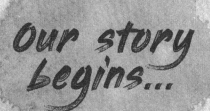

our story
begins...

Chapter 1

A Little Old Town

An elegant gradient of blue to gold stretched across a tree-filled sky, branches whipping past the bus's windows as it rumbled down the highway. Occasional dull-colored birds flittered by, their chirps echoing those of the grasshoppers perched on cattails. Small rabbits and mice scurried into thick brush, ears swiveling and noses twitching.

Christopher Korbin Faraday watched it all from his seat. He leaned heavily against the window, his breath misting the glass until, sighing, he sat up and used his sweater's sleeve to wipe it clean. The navy-blue hoodie was emblazoned with the Spectral Lakes Police Department's logo, the stylized words *SLPD*. It was a piece of clothing Chris wore with a certain amount of pride—though not enough to stop him using it to polish a window.

His headphones sat squarely on a head covered in tousled brown hair. Guitars and retro synths blared in his ears, and he held his phone rather loosely in his hand. The other rested on his backpack next to him, which contained his laptop, school books, various handheld gaming systems, and a toothbrush (with extreme mint-flavored paste). The rest of his things were in the luggage compartment below—everything he'd thought he'd need for a comfortable dorm (along with the stuff his mother insisted he bring: hairspray, cologne, and the like).

Speak of the devil: Chris's phone beeped and vibrated, the movement enough to finally send it dropping to the ground, dragging Chris's headphones and consequently his entire head with it. His forehead banged on the back of the seat in front of him. With a hiss of surprise more than pain, Chris rubbed his eyes and picked up the phone, the screen flashing with a text message.

> Mom
> Hey, are you there yet? Make sure to call us when you get there and send a picture of the dorm once you're all set up!!

With a wry smile on his face, Chris glanced back outside. The trees were melting away one by one to reveal a glistening, beautiful lake. The sun was framed between pine-laden mountains and clouds tinted with pink. Chris slid down the window and took a deep breath. Fresh mountain air. Finally.

> Chris
> Almost there. It's been a long trip. Glad you still remember me, old lady. (I'll call soon)

As the air rushed past his face, Chris felt a rising sense of hope fill him. He was beginning a new chapter, one that he alone would be able to write. *That's the point of leaving home,* he mused. *Though, really, I guess I'm returning home at the same time?*

Chris thought of the stories his grandpa used to tell. Faradays had been some of the first to strike gold in the Spectral Lake area; they'd been there during the founding of the town, and it had been Faraday-raised horses that had hauled the lumber used in the building of the town hall. The Faradays had grown famous for their beautiful and hardy steeds, but the heir to the family business, Edward Wolfram Faraday, ended up gallivanting around the world with his new bride for years on end, doing missionary work and who knows what else. The business suffered for it, and the Faraday name lost a good deal of its previous splendor. That is, until the incident.

"Edward moved the entire business to Texas after that," Grandpa Faraday had told him during Thanksgiving dinner one year. "He settled down and threw himself completely into the horse breeder's life. To this day, we have no idea what exactly happened to get him to change his tune so quickly." He grinned. "Most family thinks he murdered his wife or caused her to "go missing" for some twisted reason. I ne'er talked to him much myself. He wasn't nearl' the yappity sort of grampa I am." With that, he'd tousled Chris's hair and laughed.

Chris patted it down with a pout. "Wait, but what about your dad? Did he tell you anything?"

Grandpa Faraday shook his head. "Naw, he was just a ten-year-old boy when it happened. Maybe it's trauma or he just never knew what went down—in any case, he never talked about it. I had to squeeze the info outta other relatives. What I know for damn sure is that I never did see hide nor hair of my grandma. It was as if she never existed."

The near-empty bus rumbled to a squeaking stop at the corner of Main Street, Spectral Lakes. Chris grabbed his backpack and walked down the aisle on creaking legs, passing row after row of empty seats (save for one occupied by a sleeping older lady apparently on her way to Seattle, judging by the map in her frail hands). He nodded to the driver and the doors folded open with a squeal. Chris headed down the steps, his eyes taking in the town before him.

It was a quaint, warm-feeling place; the kind of warmth that doesn't come from the sun but from community. The kind you'd feel when your aunt took you to the county fair and bought you a caramel apple while you watched cowboys do tricks on their horses. At least, that was how Chris would describe it.

The sidewalks were made of cut and fitted wooden boards. Old-fashioned lamp posts were topped with faux gold apples. The shops lining the street weren't well-known chains but locally-owned ma and pa shops bursting with character and quirky items for sale. Down Main Street, mud-spattered trucks towed aging speed boats behind them on dusty trailers. Men wearing tackle-coated hats and fishing rods leaning against their shoulders chatted with one another by the lake, and a woman in colorful clothing watered her plants with a cat-shaped pitcher. Several rowdy teens giggled as they splashed one another in the shallows.

Framing it all was a great wooden sign propped up by two poles on either side of the street. It read:

TOWN OF SPECTRAL LAKES
EST. 1874

Gazing out at the gorgeous horizon, Chris grinned, that hopeful feeling he'd had before swelling larger within him.

He took the rest of his luggage from the bus's undercarriage—a large suitcase and a guitar case covered in hand-drawn musical notes and hearts in permanent marker (this was the doing of his "hilarious" little sister). He'd covered the most embarrassing doodles with pieces of duct tape.

On the sidewalk, Chris opened the suitcase and fished for the not-so-carefully folded map he'd bought during his last visit. His fingers brushed the printed streets, framed on one side by Lake Spectral and on the other by the smaller lakes Kelpie and Lullaby. Crowgold National Park took up a good portion of the space beyond Lake Spectral, and most of the land around Kelpie and Lullaby was dedicated to apple farming or lumber (industries the town had thrown itself into after the gold dried up). A red circle a way south of his position marked Foxglove University and its

nearby dormitories.

Luggage in tow, He made his way down Main Street toward the lake. The water stretched out in front of him, azure and blue, and he paused for a moment to breathe the cool air. Continuing on down the wooden sidewalk, he passed multitudes of friendly folk who greeted him with warm smiles, some asking him if he was visiting or if he needed help carrying his stuff. He waved back and politely declined assistance.

As the sun dipped lower on the horizon, Chris spotted a Stop N' Go fast food joint on a street corner. He made a beeline for the place, pausing suddenly as he passed a small tourist shop. It was a small building, as quaint as anything in town, and displayed behind its windows was a miniature version of Lake Spectral, complete with real water, gravel, and cute little pine trees made of carved and painted wood. Miniature houses and tiny plastic people dotted the shore. The scene would have been striking enough alone—but, "floating" on a track beneath the lake's surface, a small glass woman in an old-style dress circled the water, her janky movements adding to the discomfort that settled over Chris like a blanket. A small fog machine puffed occasionally, steam rolling across the water's surface. The sign above the display read:

> *Spectral Lakes: Home to The REAL Lady of the Lake!*
> *FREE Sighting Guide Inside!*

Several shelves around the model lake held all manner of things—plushies, books, key chains, and snow globes—all of them dedicated to the ghostly woman. Chris eyed a notebook emblazoned with the face of a tattered, sickly green mermaid pockmarked with oozing bullet holes. Beside it, a postcard depicted an upstanding gentlewoman, her skin blue and translucent, her eyes black and deep.

Every small town needs a cryptid to bring in tourists, Chris thought. *Instead of a cute sea lizard or silly alien, this one went for a deadly ghost siren. Charming.*

Chris had seen a few depictions of the Lady when he'd last visited, during last year's Fall

Festival. He'd spent a little while pondering the birth of the legend, but something about this particular spirit made him unreasonably nervous. He shivered and turned away. The neon sign of Stop N' Go buzzed into life as the sun dipped below the dark, distant mountains.

Stomach full of burger and forehead laced with sweat, Chris finally made it to his dorm. With a heavy sigh of relief, he unlocked his door to reveal a small square room that contained two loft beds with simple desks and shelving units beneath.

At the desk on the right, a scrawny guy with oily black hair was glued to his computer screen. In fact, it seemed as if his LED-encrusted custom gaming PC and all of its accessories were the only things he'd unpacked so far. Various unopened cardboard boxes and suitcases were scattered around him and, on-screen, an FPS game was unfolding; Chris guessed it was *Call of Battle* or some other title with the same brown-grey generic military theme.

Chris watched him for a moment before

waving. "Hey, there!" he said.

The guy blinked but didn't respond until his character got shotgunned point-blank by an enemy lurking in the bushes. He cried out in frustration and whipped his head around to face Chris. His scowl faded as his eyes slipped down to Chris's SLPD hoodie.

"A criminal justice guy," he muttered, rolling his eyes. "Of all the shitty people to room with..."

Chris blinked. "Uh... okay?" He threw his bag toward the free bunk, his nose wrinkled in disgust. "I get it. We'll mutually pretend the other doesn't exist."

The guy was already back to his game.

Chris unpacked quickly, setting up his things on the desk and shelves. When he was done, he took a picture of the place for his mom, crashed on his bed, and threw off his hoodie. He played on his handheld for about a half hour before drifting to sleep, the game's tinny music playing softly until the console died. The moon's light shone through the windows, bathing a stray newspaper sheet leftover from the roommate's packing.

The Spectral Lakes Chronicle

Sept. 14th, 2009

LADY OF THE LAKE OR DEMON OF DEATH?

*New paranormal figure photographed by jour-
nalist Frank Shores! A pure black figure with
glowing red eyes... could it be the Lady, or something even more sinister? Details inside!*

Chapter 2
The Girl

The next day started rather miserably. Chris was sore from his journey, and pretty damn tired to boot. He dragged himself out of bed, ignored his roommate (who, somehow, was *still* playing his game), dressed, grabbed his laptop bag, and set out to find somewhere that sold a good cup of coffee. That is, if he could find one.

He spotted a fellow student—a tall guy with red-brown hair— heading into the dorms. In his pale arms, he cradled a full coffee tumbler.

"Hey," Chris called, jogging to catch up. "Do you know anywhere I could get good coffee?"

The student stopped, turning to face Chris. "Oh," he said, grinning, "Sure! The coffee in the common room is terrible—if you want the good stuff, most of us go to Citron Cafe. It's over on Lockwood street."

"Thanks!"

"No problem." The red-haired guy stood awkwardly for a moment before giving a shy smile. "So, err, I gotta get to class, but I hope you enjoy it."

Chris waved and started away toward Lockwood street. His hopes for the day were a little brighter now that he'd met a friendly face.

The Citron Cafe turned out to be a cute little place whose lemon-yellow and white exterior looked like something out of a Broadway Victorian musical. Inside it was all warm, chocolatey browns and creams, with hints of the same yellow as outside. Chris wanted to settle into one of the huge leather chairs near the fireplace with a good book or two, but his first class started in a half hour and he wasn't looking to be late on the first day, no matter how tempting it was.

He got a cup of black coffee and took a sip. Immediately his posture straightened, eyes widened, and a smile spread across his face. *Good stuff.*

Back outside, the full force of the morning sun blazed down upon him. Blinking, he turned away, trying to shield himself with his arm. Ahead, sitting at a small picnic table, was a girl, her pale face and straight blonde hair glowing in the warm light. She was buried in a book with French phrases on the cover and, in her free hand, she absent-mindedly twirled a spoon around her coffee mug. She wore a loose pink crop-top emblazoned with a swan and the word *Cygne*. Her long legs elegantly crossed one another, one of her feet bouncing gently in time with the dim music leaking from her earbuds. It sounded like...

Is that screamo? Chris blinked, suddenly snapping away

from the picturesque scene. He recognized the song she was listening to, too. It was "Phoenix Caw" by Vincent Firestar. One of Chris's siblings, Katie, had gotten super into screamo in her emo phase. The entire Faraday family had been desperately thankful when she finally grew out of it. What remained was Chris's involuntary knowledge of songs he never wanted to hear blasting out of his sister's room at midnight ever again.

Still, the girl was... *very* pretty, and her out-of-place music taste only cemented her image in Chris's mind as he walked away from her and down the street toward Foxglove U.

The rest of the day passed slowly but gently enough. Lectures were full of syllabus read-alouds and lengthy PowerPoints put together by professors not familiar with the idea of visual aids. In between classes, Chris ate snacks, typed up song ideas on his laptop, and chatted with a few classmates at length about upcoming game releases (things got a bit heated when they brought out their handhelds and battled one another. Chris almost got a water bottle to the face when he beat a guy in a Foxglove letterman. It was all in good fun, though. At least, that's what he'd insisted).

It was only when Chris sat down for his five o'clock algebra class that the day's activities started to get to him. He was pretty sure he could actually *feel* the last vestiges of caffeine seeping from his veins. He slumped gradually lower in his seat, head leaning on one hand, eyelids quivering in the low light... The lecturer, a shriveled man who looked like a naked mole rat, droned on about cell phone policies and late work submissions.

Chris's head lowered by another degree and, for the second time that day, sunlight caught in his eyes. Suppressing a groan, he rubbed his face and glanced, red-eyed, at the window. The late afternoon sun framed the figure of a girl, light haloing her pale hair.

Wait a freakin' minute. Chris rubbed his eyes again. *Hey, it's* her *again.*

There she sat at the edge of the classroom, earbuds still in, face still in her book. She had a bag of mint candies partially hidden in her purse, and every so often she'd cover her face with her book and stealthily pop one into her mouth.

Her gaze wandered from her book and, for a brief moment, her eyes caught Chris's. Cheeks glowing, Chris turned away.

Citron Cafe must be popular with students. Either that or this is a very fortunate coincidence. He stole a look at her again before burying his nose in his algebra textbook. She... really was pretty. *I should talk to her after class or—nah. No. I need to take a shower or something.* He nervously glanced at his T-shirt, checking for sweat stains. *Maybe Mom's extra packing wasn't such a bad idea after all.*

His phone lightly buzzed, a message popping up on-screen.

Nick
You all settled in yet? Was thinking we could grab some Stop N' Go and hang out!

Chris perked up. He hid his phone behind an open textbook and typed out a reply.

Chris
Yeah! Let's do it. Maybe at 8?

Nick
Sure, see you there.

A mother crow shot down from a purple sky littered with stars. She snatched a long, soggy french fry from the sidewalk and swooped upward, landing in the little nest she'd built on the dazzling Stop N' Go sign.

Chris watched as she dropped the fry into the waiting mouths of her children. He raised his phone and took a photo. His dad was a bit of a bird nut (alongside being a horse nut), so Chris sent it to him. He leaned against one of the fast food joint's windows and peered out over the neighboring lake. The placid water glittered beyond the glowing shopfronts of Lakeside Road.

A small car pulled to a stop near Chris. The headlights snapped off and two figures stepped out. One was a big guy—maybe six feet tall or more, and very fit. He wore a polo shirt and dress pants, and his black hair was slicked back. With him was a young woman, her bright red hair pulled into a ponytail. She looked small compared to the man, but was really around Chris's height. She adjusted her brown leather jacket and glanced at Chris with what he interpreted as indifference.

"Chris! Hey, glad to see you!" the man called as he waved.

"Hey, Nick!" Chris grinned, giving him a friendly fistbump. "Nice to see you too."

"Glad the trip all the way up here was all right." Nick looked around, his brows raising. "Say, did you walk all the way here from campus?"

"Yeah, why?"

"Oh, geez! If I'd known, I would have

offered you a ride." Nick grimaced, rubbing the back of his head. "Hey, I've got an old bike you can have if you want."

"Sure—!"

"He really shouldn't be wandering around at night in the first place," the woman started, her

gaze flickering to the road behind her.

Nick sighed. "Oh, come on. Don't scare him." He gave Chris a sympathetic look. "Nothing bad happens around here. We'd know. We've had to file the paperwork... or lack thereof."

"I see," Chris said slowly, frowning slightly at the woman.

A moment passed. Both the woman and Chris stared at Nick expectantly. His eyes widened.

"*Oh!* I forgot to introduce you two!" He gave a quick laugh before motioning to his companion. "Chris, this is Ms. Esther Quinn. She's my partner in our latest case. I thought she might want to eat with us."

"I'm hungry," stated Esther in a bored tone.

"Uh, nice to meet you." Chris reached to shake her hand.

"Charmed," she said, returning the shake, a slight smile on her lips but her eyes still hooded.

"Sooooo..." Chris slowly turned to face Nick, grinning. "You mentioned a case?"

"Aw, can't tell you much, I'm afraid," Nick

said regretfully, his hand once again scratching the back of his head. "Some work info is private while we're working on it. I'd need to get permission to—"

"Just a bunch of kids spray-painting lewd jargon on state park road signs. That's it." Esther rolled her eyes.

"*Esther!*" Nick cried. A few of the hairs that had been so meticulously smoothed back came loose and fell over his forehead.

"Let's eat now, K?" Esther said, the corners of her mouth curling up.

Nick gave her an indignant glare before slumping his shoulders with a sigh. "Fine."

The group settled into one of the booths, Nick and Esther crowding in on one side while Chris sat on the other. The window next to them glared with artificial light and, behind it, the soft white of the moon.

Esther plunged face-first into her burger, while Nick took bites of a tomato salad and Chris intermittently switched between his cheeseburger and fries.

"So, it's been nice to have more time to

spend with Faye," Nick went on. "After the honeymoon, we had so much work that it was hard to just be together."

"Wow, it must be tough when you both work such crazy hours," Chris said between bites.

Nick waved an impaled piece of tomato around on his fork. "I'm telling you, her schedule is *insane*. It's like the hospital is her *real* home."

"And yours is at your desk in the station playing *Guild of Swordcraft* and *Legends of Valkyrie* while scarfing down donuts, right?" Chris smirked, giving Nick a knowing look.

"Hey, you're the one with the paper-white skin here, man," Nick remarked with a chuckle, pointing his fork at his accuser. "If anyone's been gaming twenty-four-seven, it's you."

Esther glanced between them. "Hey, how'd you two meet, anyway?"

Nick took a sip of water before acknowledging her with a smile. "I visited Texas to see family and met him at a church there. We ended up playing *Legends of Valkyrie* and joining the same guild."

Esther cocked her head. "So you're gamer bros. Got it." Her tone was unreadable, Chris thought—it lacked enthusiasm, but she didn't seem disinterested either.

"Well, we ended up talking about his job and how I'd been wanting to become an officer," Chris explained. "He told me about the program at Foxglove, so last summer I came up here to check it out during the town festival."

Esther smirked, a few fries sticking out of her mouth like cigarettes. "You mean the day our only working fire truck crashed into a hotdog stand and started a fire?"

Chris glanced upward, cringing internally at the recollection. "Yep, that's the one... It sure was an *interesting* day." He looked down at his jacket, spreading his arms to show it off. "But, before that, I took a tour of the station and got this free hoodie. I've been wearing it a lot ever since."

"Oh. Well, if you ever wear that one out, we've got piles of 'em leftover in the evidence locker," Esther said, focused once again on her food. "There's not really much else in there."

Chris's shoulders slumped slightly. "Uh... I see."

Nick looked at Esther disapprovingly. "Esther, lighten up on the kid. He's *actually* excited about this line of work." He winked at Chris. "It's refreshing after spending the day with *you* as my partner."

Chris couldn't help laughing, though he covered his mouth so he didn't cough food all over the table. Nick joined in. This time, it was easy to read Esther's emotions: she wasn't amused.

It had been over a year since Chris had seen Nick. Now, laughing with him in a burger joint, Chris realized how nice it was to spend time with a friend again. That was one of the reasons he'd moved all the way up to this little town: to start anew, sure, but also to have good people he could rely on. He'd never had a friend let him down before.

"Are you sure you don't want a ride back to your dorm?" Nick asked, one foot already inside his car as he leaned against the open door.

"Nah, I like the walk. I *will* take you up on

that bike proposition though."

"All right man, you do you. See ya in Valhalla tomorrow!"

"Oh yeah, the fall event is starting, right? That means a new skin for my support main!" Chris exclaimed.

"You bet! And there's a new game mode that lowers mana costs for the entire match and makes cooldowns—"

"What on earth are you talking about?" Esther pursed her lips.

"Oh, uh, *Legends of Valkyrie* stuff." Nick turned to Chris. "Bye, man!" And with that, he closed the car door and drove off.

Chris buried his hands in his pockets as an unnervingly chill breeze rustled his hair. Maybe he should have taken Nick's offer, he thought.

Movement from a few buildings down caught his eye. A ballet studio was closing for the night, a few women and a man waving goodbyes to one another and heading toward their cars. A lone girl came out, a sequined ballet bag glittering in her arms as she stood under a street lamp. She yawned and stretched, running a hand through her messy bun before pulling a thick jacket over her leotard.

Chris's breath caught in his throat and he had to force himself to not hack out a cough.

Her again!? How on earth...?

He watched as she gracefully walked down the road toward a parking lot. He felt words clutter his mouth but wouldn't let himself release them. Ambushing a woman walking alone at night wasn't the best way to introduce yourself.

Why do I keep seeing her everywhere? God, if she sees me, please don't let her think I'm some kinda stalker.

He grimaced and pulled his hood over his head, hurrying in the opposite direction.

What is going on...? Am I just going to keep running into her until I say something?

"Good job, Faraday..." Chris scoffed to himself under his breath.

Cold wind buffeted his jacket and he allowed himself to stop. Sighing, he gazed out over the lake. He froze.

There was someone there. Standing on the water. Way out in the middle of the lake.

Chris's brows knitted together. He stepped forward, trying to get a better look.

It wasn't just a trick of the light—there was definitely someone there. A woman, shrouded in mist, in a dull blue dress. But... something wasn't right. He couldn't see her face, but her body was turned toward him, as if her head was craned like an owl's... as if...

Chris's skin crawled as if coated in spiders. His gut twisted as he stumbled back.

In a swift motion, her head turned to face him. Even from here, Chris could see the empty black holes where her eyes should have been.

Gradually, she raised a bony arm. One of her long fingers unfurled. It was pointing at him.

Her mouth opened, black water pouring from it down her dress. Her lips moved.

"What's wrong, did ya see the Lady of the Lake or something?" Uttered a playful voice just behind Chris.

He screamed and whipped around to see the ballet girl standing there. "Oh, God! I'm so sorry!" she said with a nervous laugh, "if I'd known you were that wound up, I wouldn't have snuck up on you. Are you okay?"

Chris glanced back at the lake, scanning the dark horizon. The figure was gone. He pulled heavy breaths into his lungs, the cold air chilling him from the inside out. He struggled to meet the girl's eyes.

"I just... I thought I saw something... Jesus..."

"You thought you saw Jesus? I've been waiting for his return too, but I'm not seeing fire in the sky so I guess it's a false alarm. Bummer."

"Huh?"

"I was making a joke about wanting the world to end." She paused, examining his face. "Yikes, you really got the shit scared out of you, didn't ya? Uh, sorry for joking again. I hoped it'd relieve the tension." She gave him a concerned look, her gaze trading between him and the lake. "Did you see the Lady? I think you're new around here so I don't know if you've heard about her or not. She's kind of a tourism thing but..." she trailed off before her eyes bored into his. "Well? Did you?"

Chris gazed back, his breath coming back to him. "I—I don't know. It sounds kinda stupid."

The girl fidgeted with her ballet bag. "It's not. I've seen her too. Long time ago. Thought I was crazy!" She shrugged. "It's all right—really. I want to know."

Chris blinked, his body still buzzed on adrenalin. "Yeah," he said at last. "I think I saw her. It was so... vivid." His shoulders slumped. "Oh, and, uh, I don't get high or any of that. Is this, like, a common illusion people here see or what? Like a particular way the moon casts light through the trees onto the water?"

"Dude, you're just trying to rationalize it now. Don't lose the fun. *I* think she's real, at least." The girl held up her keyring, upon which was a little Lady of the Lake plastic charm. "She hardly comes out, though. Sightings that vivid are super rare. You're lucky."

Chris didn't *feel* lucky.

"By the way, I saw you in Algebra this afternoon. Looks like we're classmates, huh?" She smiled. "I'm Charlotte 'Sorry to Have Scared You Shitless' Ramsey. Nice to formally meet you."

Her smile sent a flood of red to Chris's cheeks. He felt a lot warmer now. His posture finally relaxed and a genuine smile appeared on his lips.

"I'm Chris 'Scaredy-Pants' Faraday. Yeah, I saw you earlier too. Wanted to talk to you but I— uh—"

"It's okay, I have that effect on people." She fluttered her eyelashes and chuckled. "Nah, I get it." She glanced at his hoodie. "So, I'm assuming you're in the criminal justice track?"

Chris nodded. "I've always had a passion for justice and all that stuff. Watched a bunch of superhero cartoons and crime dramas growing up. Always stuck with me, I guess. What are you majoring in?"

"Aw, that's cool! I'm going into education and language types of things. My real love is ballet but, if that doesn't work out, I want to be an English teacher in France. Always wanted to live there someday." The corners of her smile dimpled.

"Now those are nice dreams. Very chic."

Charlotte checked her watch. "Oh, I better get home. Classes tomorrow. It was really nice meeting you, even under strange circumstances." She nodded at him.

"Oh, definitely! And—yeah, thanks for helping me calm down. I, uh, will probably be having nightmares tonight." He gave a nervous chuckle.

"Yup. Make sure your sleep self says hi to the Lady for me. Tell her I'm a fan." Charlotte winked. "Well, bye, Chris 'Spotter of Ghosts' Faraday!"

"See you around, Charlotte 'Lady of the Lake' Ramsey!" Chris grinned and waved as she began to walk away. "Wait! Uh, do you want to meet at Citron Cafe or something before class?"

Charlotte looked back, a hand brushing away stray hairs from her rich brown eyes. "Sounds good to me! See you then."

Her smile stayed in Chris's mind all the way home. It was infectious and, even as he climbed into bed, he couldn't stop grinning.

As soon as he drifted into sleep, however, his smile faded.

His nightmares were visceral. He was being drowned in the lake, a woman with long, stringy white hair and empty pits for eyes using stony arms to push him under the black water. He heard a different woman call his name over and over. She pleaded for him to answer. She was crying.

His lungs filled with water.

Yet somehow he uttered a single word.

"*Eleanor!*"

Chapter 3
Blossoming Forth

The first date with Charlotte went exceptionally well. Then the next, and the next, and the next. Soon, they were sitting beside one another in every shared class, eating breakfast together every day at Citron Cafe, arguing about whether the movies they saw were actually good, and helping one another with homework. Chris attended her ballet practices and watched her as she danced. She was graceful in all her movements—like a swan gliding across a lake, he thought. Chris would sit next to one of the mirror walls with his laptop open, his attention supposedly focused on his homework but his eyes telling another story.

While Charlotte's job was to teach kids the basics of dance, Chris ended up part-timing at Citron Cafe and, in his spare time, making music to post online. He set up a recording studio of sorts in his exceptionally small dorm closet and played guitar. When he showed some of his work to Charlotte, her eyes widened and, at her eager suggestion, she ended up practicing to his songs.

On Chris's birthday late in the fall, she gifted him a small blue ukulele. On Saturday evenings they'd rent a boat and sail out into the middle of the lake, Chris softly strumming the instrument while Charlotte rested her head in his lap and hummed along, her fingers tracing abstract shapes in the water's surface. Sometimes she'd sing in French; songs like "*La Vie en Rose*" and "*Les Roses Blanches*." For Chris, those moments seemed to stop time. Everything felt so *right*.

Sometimes they would go to Crowgold National Park and hike the wild trails. One afternoon, they climbed up Mount Faraday and took pictures at the edge of Redford Cliff, which overlooked the lake and, on its far shore, the entire town.

"The mountain is named after my family, you know," Chris revealed with a smirk as he put away his photo-laden phone. "Buncha our horses used to live on the slopes."

"Ooooo!" Charlotte cooed. She sat on the cliff's edge and gazed around the girth of the enormous mountain. "You have some real history with this place, huh?"

Chris sat beside her. "Yeah. I bet there's like a horse graveyard up here or something. Some ghost mare is probably gonna haunt me for getting turned into glue."

Charlotte rolled her eyes before resting her head on his shoulder. They both let the moment sit for a while.

"So... what scares you?" Charlotte asked. Her fingers drummed against his thigh.

"Where did that come from?" Chris took a swig from his water bottle.

"I saw a bunch of old cheesy horror flicks at the movie rental place. Thought it would be fun to marathon them sometime. Now reveal to me your secrets, ancient one!" She waved her hand before him in a mystical fashion.

"Your wish is my command." Chris responded in a deep voice that ended in a hacking cough. "Uhhm. Huh. I can't say I've thought about it that often."

"Not many people really want to know their deepest fears. Plus, it's hard to know unless you've experienced it. But it's interesting to think about, right?"

"Are you a psychiatrist now?" Chris shook his head with a smile. "But yeah, you're right. I wonder if anyone can really fear anything unless they've experienced it. Like"—he motioned to the cliff's edge—"I'm scared of falling off the edge but, if I've never actually fallen off of something and hurt myself, I don't really know what it is I'm afraid of. Does that make sense?"

Charlotte cocked her head. "Yeah. Now enough talk. Spill it."

Chris took a deep breath. "All right. It's drowning."

"Aha! So why is it that you swim in the lake just fine eh, Faraday?"

Chris pushed a hand through his sweat-slick hair. "Calm down. I'll tell you the story." He adjusted himself and gazed out at the lake. Somehow, the water's fresh, calming scent reached them from the surface below.

"So, one day my family and I went out to

swim at the beach in Galveston—that's a city at the Gulf of Mexico. We set up the towels and umbrellas and everything before my siblings headed into the water. Mom and Dad stayed behind to watch Sarah and Walter—they were babies at the time—while my sister Katie and I were tasked with watching the others."

"How old were you?"

"Twelve."

"Ooh, that's a lot of responsibility for a kiddo."

"That's how it is when you've got a lot of siblings. You have to step up, you know? Partly to help Mom"—Chris shrugged—"and partly to get more allowance. You know, the important things in life."

Charlotte nodded. "Oh, of course. I'm sure the action figures were worth it."

"Hey, being able to buy *Guild of Swordcraft* on release was worth changing Walter's diaper."

"A life-changing experience, I'm sure."

"Are you gonna keep sassing me or am I gonna finish this story?"

Charlotte smirked, her head on his shoulder. "Oh, please, continue."

"I went out and swam in the waves. Made sure to keep an eye out for Clara, the youngest—she was still getting the hang of resisting the waves' pull. It was a fun time. We all ran out with our bodyboards and had a blast."

"But?"

"*But* then I saw a few teenage girls in bikinis on the shore."

Charlotte could barely hold back her guffaws. "Oh my God. What did you do?"

Chris sucked breath through his teeth, trying to bury his smile. "I was twelve, all right? I thought I was the peak of masculinity."

"What did you do, Chris?"

"Well, first, I tried bodyboarding, like, *really* impressively. Something that would catch their eyes. It didn't work."

"No shit."

"Kid brain, Charlotte! Kid brain! When that failed, I walked up onto the shore and leaned against the board like I was posing for an action movie or something. That didn't work either. It was time for my last resort. I walked up to them, fully prepared to recite, line for line, one of the pick-up lines from a James Bond film I'd just seen."

Charlotte had her hands over her face.

"But before I could embarrass myself to an *unprecedented* degree, I noticed that I couldn't see Clara anywhere. Not in the water, not on the beach. I panicked—bad. I ran into the water and tried searching around for her. I asked Katie if she's seen her. She hadn't. Katie went to get Mom and Dad while I went farther out into the water."

Charlotte's suppressed giggles had stopped.

"I kept feeling around in the waves and diving under with my goggles to try to see her. I got so far out in the water that there weren't many other kids around. In fact, I noticed that I was out much farther than I'd thought. I tried swimming back, but that made it worse. I was caught in a riptide.

"In my panic, I forgot what the signs around the beach said to do in that situation. I floundered around, trying to break away from the water's force. I got out a few cries for help before a huge wave crashed over my head and sent me spiraling underwater. The sand whipped up into my eyes—I couldn't see anything. I didn't know which way was up. My lungs sucked in water, and my vision was going black.

"That's when I felt a small hand grab my own. In that heartbeat, I could tell it was Clara. All of a sudden there was this... feeling? It's hard to describe. I *couldn't* let us both drown. My body refused to. I oriented myself and finally broke through the surface of the water, coughing up all the crap I'd swallowed. I pulled Clara up after me. She was barely conscious.

"Katie and Dad were calling for us desperately. When they saw us, they practically dragged the lifeguard with them. I felt a rush of relief but also... how to say this... a burning feeling? Every moment I was in the water, I felt like it would suck me back in and make me helpless again. I was, uh, crying pretty bad." He grinned suddenly, his face cracking. "No hope of getting a girl anymore."

Charlotte gave a small smile.

"So, Clara and I got medical attention and everything turned out okay. But, after that, I had a phobia of deep water and the ocean for a long while. It was years until I was able to go to the deep end of the pool again. I also was a little... *overly protective* of Clara."

"That's sweet... oh, not the whole ordeal, I mean, but the way you took care of your sister," Charlotte said quickly.

"I didn't want to see her be hurt, especially not because I'd messed up. It was a bit of a wake-up call to what's really important, I guess."

"Your family?"

"Yeah. And doing the best with the time

you've got."

"Deep."

"You asked."

Charlotte wove her fingers between his. "That's the real reason you want to be an officer, isn't it? It's not just superhero cartoons and crime shows. You want to be able to take responsibility and help people."

"I guess so."

Charlotte smiled. "That's cute."

"I'm glad you find my hero backstory quaintly charming." Chris took another swig of water.

"If I didn't find you charming, I wouldn't be here, dumbass." Charlotte dangled her legs over the cliff's edge. "Though I gotta say, you're not so much the Prince Charming type as you are the goody-two-shoes boy scout type."

"Uh... that's good, right? I didn't get the Eagle Scout rank for nothing." He puffed out his chest, his jaw set.

"Oh my God, shut up." Charlotte playfully punched his arm. "You see, I'm playing the long game. Someday, when we're middle-aged, you'll be a grizzled, hard-boiled cop with a coffee always in-hand and the perfect amount of stubble on your chin. Not to mention the ever-present harsh noir shadows keeping your face angular. That's sexy."

"At least I know what you're into now. I finally have an ideal to live up to."

"And what do you want from me, eh? Should I become the classic femme fatale to match?"

"Nah. You're fine as is."

"Whenever guys say that, they're lying."

"Fine..." Chris paused. "A little less sass would be nice."

Charlotte stopped, her mouth open. "Shit. I can't respond to that. Anything clever would just prove your point. Damnit."

"Glad to know I can take your breath away."

"Chris! Stop it! That's dad-joke level. We're not there yet."

"All right, all right..."

They sat there for just a while longer, waiting for the cool spill of evening shadows before rising and heading back to the trail. There was a particular feeling in the pine-scented air—Chris could only describe it as the sensation of *home*.

On the one-year anniversary of Chris's arrival in Spectral Lakes, the couple attended the Spectral Lakes Fall Festival. It was a beautiful night, warm and balmy, and the festival lights flooded the trees. Carnival games, copious amounts of snacks, and local crafts filled the evening.

At one point, the two of them stopped by a wood carving booth operated by a friendly man coated in sawdust. He taught Chris the basics of carving, handing him a small knife and a block of wood marked with a bird's shape in pencil. He left Chris to it and attended to the next customer.

As his knife scraped against soft wood, Chris leaned back against the side of the booth. Charlotte, he could see, was watching his busy hands. He glanced to the next booth over—the owner of the local tourist shop, a beaming, wide-faced woman, was passing out flyers and free Lady of the Lake keychains to those who would listen to her sales spiel.

Charlotte smirked and snaked her arm around Chris's elbow. "Fun fact. That lady dated my dad in high school, you know. Her name's Veronica Shores."

"Really, now?"

"Yeah, apparently she was just as weird as she is today. Always talking her head off about business ideas and her seven dogs. She's a good person, though—helps out at the animal shelter a lot."

"Wanna know another fun fact?" Chris asked, his blade rasping against the slowly form-ing wooden bird.

"What would that be?"

"Most cruise ships have morgues on them for the people who die on board. Sometimes su-per old couples will spend their savings on cruis-ing until they die. Like, they think it's a good way to go out or something."

"Romantic."

"You really think so, or are you just pulling my leg?"

"Nah, it's actually kinda neat. I'd rather they just throw my corpse overboard, though. I can bear being fish food. Circle of life and all that jazz." Charlotte twirled a finger in the air.

"I'd rather have my ashes be fertilizer for the oak tree in front of my family's house. I used to climb up it to hide from Katie. I'd keep a supply of snacks and books in the branches."

"Can't you also have your ashes to be compressed into a diamond these days? That sounds cool. Maybe it could be put on a ring."

"Sounds like a morbid way of getting engaged to a ghost."

Charlotte's eyes lit up. "Oh, that reminds me. My turn for fact time again. So, I found out that there are old legends about ghost investigators in this area—people who would go out and try to dissipate spirits, guide them to the afterlife, that kinda thing. Found out about it from one of Veronica's brochures." She glanced at the Lady keychain hanging from her purse. "Wonder if they gave up on exorcizing the Lady years ago. Creepy stuff."

"Damnit—!" Chris fumbled with the knife.

Charlotte raised an eyebrow. "What's wrong?"

"Cut myself." He sucked on his index finger for a moment before examining it. "I'm fine."

Charlotte pulled a tissue from her purse and helped wrap the wound. "Hey, your little bird is looking cute!" She took it up in her hands. It was simple, but at least recognizable.

"Thanks. Maybe I'll keep this up. It's relaxing." Chris paused to look at his phone. "It's late. We should head to the lakeside."

"Why?"

"Well, I thought you might want to join in on the Lakeside Dance with me."

Charlotte blinked. "Isn't that a somewhat, well, *formal* event?" She motioned to her skinny jeans and crop top. "Not saying I'm never *not* the belle of the ball, but..."

Chris took off his backpack and unzipped it. He pulled out a folded suit and one of Charlotte's party dresses. He snapped a finger and gave what he hoped was a dashing smile. "I'm always prepared."

Charlotte pressed the dress against her chest. "Chris. I gotta say. This is impressive. But at the same time, I want to hurt you for folding this and stuffing it in a backpack."

"Can that wait 'til after the dance?"

Charlotte tapped a finger against her chin. "I *guess.*"

Chris adjusted his tie one final time and emerged from the men's room to find Charlotte decked out in a long evening gown. Defying the laws of time, she'd somehow already completely redone her makeup, and now looked as sharp and elegant as ever.

Arm in arm, the two headed for the beach.

The dance floor was already busy. Above, the low moon hung like a silver pendulum, and sweeping music by local swing musicians led the pair off their feet; they twirled along the gravel as if afloat on the writhing mist of the water's surface. The band began to play "*Two Sleepy Peo-*

ple," and an old crooner in a peacock-blue suit stepped up to the mic.

The pair swayed, entwined in one another's arms. Charlotte nestled her head into Chris's shoulder. Around them, the dancers turned into colorful blurs. The yellow-white lights strung through the trees illuminated Charlotte's brown eyes.

Chris really *loved* her. He loved her laugh, her eyes, the way her hair spilled down her back, her long legs and the way she moved, her vibrant personality, her everything.

She turned her head to look up at him. His breath caught. They stood on a small boardwalk by the lake, the water lapping against the sides, the moon unreal, everything gentle—and Charlotte moved closer, her hand finding his cheek. As if gravity had suddenly taken hold of them, their faces slowly drifted together, lips intertwining.

Once they parted, their gazes met. Charlotte couldn't help but give a thrilled giggle, her fingers tightening around Chris's shoulder. He laughed in kind.

"I love you, Charlotte Ramsey," he

breathed.

"God, I love you, too, Christopher Faraday."

To Chris's ears, those were the most beautiful words ever spoken.

In December, they flew down to Texas to join the Faraday family festivities, which, Chris assured Charlotte, were always over the top and involved the whole Faraday clan; plenty of presents; and rich, homemade food.

"Are you sure you wouldn't rather spend the week with your family? I don't want to steal you away from them for the holidays," Chris had said while they discussed their vacation plans.

Charlotte paused a moment. "My parents aren't around anymore," she explained as she picked at grass along the lakeshore. "They died on a missions trip when I was a teen. Some kind of fire in the place they were staying. The smoke got to them."

Christopher's brows rose. "I'm—I'm sorry."

Charlotte shrugged. "Thankfully they

didn't feel a thing. And besides, my dad would have been watching you the entire visit—probably while making threatening gestures." She donned a nostalgic smile. "You really would have had to prove yourself to him."

"I would have liked to meet him," Chris said sincerely, "And tell him he raised a wonderful daughter."

"Well I hope you aren't expecting me to tell your parents the same." Charlotte winked.

Chris found he couldn't really respond to that, not after the sobering news. So he simply smiled and went on with the planning.

He was able to introduce Charlotte to pretty much his entire family. His parents adored her, all five of his siblings thought she was "pretty cool," and his aunts, uncles, and cousins were "very pleased to meet her." When she met Grandpa Faraday, however, something a little strange happened.

"This is Charlotte Ramsey, my girlfriend," Chris explained to the old man with a smile.

Grandpa smiled wildly, taking her hand in both of his and joyfully shaking, but when Charlotte was called into the living room to receive her gift basket, he took Chris aside.

"She's a Ramsey, right? She lives in Spectral Lakes?" Grandpa Faraday's mustache was twitching.

"Yeah, she's lived there her whole life. What's wrong?" Chris tilted his head.

Grandpa rubbed his beard, his eyes glazing over as if they were traveling back to that lakeside town. His lips moved as if to say something, but he kept cutting himself off. "Ramsey..."

The old man was quiet for the rest of the night. He looked as if he was trying hard to remember something important.

At first, Chris was concerned but, as the party continued and he mingled with more of his family, the incident slipped from his mind. Spending the holidays with everyone he loved left him feeling as if he were walking on air.

After everyone was full of Christmas dinner and lounging together in the living room, it was time for a bit of homegrown entertainment. Chris's mother Caroline swept into the room, her overly tinseled dress matching her sparkling eyes.

Behind her trailed Clara, Sarah, and Walter, all dressed in matching red velvet clothes and looking utterly embarrassed. Nevertheless, at their mother's insistence (and Chris's silent hand motions of "Do this or else Mom is gonna be sad") they sang carols in harmony before the crackling fireplace.

Next up were the middle children, Peter and Steven. They were in their late teens now, and their refusal to sing in front of the family had led them to propose indoor skateboarding tricks instead. Both their mother and father had vetoed this, so the two resorted to giving an impromptu presentation about the morality of forcing children to perform in front of family. It even included detailed sources.

Caroline wasn't amused, but Chris's father Richard and the rest of the family were doubled over in laughter at the various home video clips the boys brought in as evidence, which included Aunt Becky tap dancing and Richard's first time riding a horse. Not even their fellow siblings were spared. Katie gasped in horror when an old video of her singing in the bathroom was played, and

Sarah pouted as she fell down on-screen during a ballet recital. And, to Chris's complete mortification, the entire family was subjected to an old recording entitled "Chris's Mysteries!" in which a seven-year-old, gap-toothed little Faraday filmed his own murder mystery show. This included several ketchup-coated action figures screaming as they were stabbed by a butter knife-wielding, black-cloaked Barbie doll covered in permanent marker tattoos. Charlotte was laughing so hysterically she had to leave the room for a full minute.

After the horror show of events had passed, it was Chris's turn to entertain. The previous act was hard to follow but, nonetheless, he strapped his guitar around his shoulder and stood before the fireplace, Charlotte at his side. Hand brushing the taut strings, he began to play. Together, he and Charlotte sang an old Faraday tune passed down from the days of Spectral Lakes. In the corner, Grandpa Faraday sat in a leather chair, gazing deep into the wine swirling in his glass.

When you go crying
And run into the night
Don't ever be
Ever be
Out of my sight

Once you kiss me sweetly
You'll never be free
For our love's a chain
Made of sea
Made of sea

And in hand
Your heart at my command
And in faith
These bonds keep us safe

These bonds keep us safe...

A lifetime of Sunday services with his family had left its mark on Chris, and he'd found a church in Spectral Lakes shortly after settling in. It was a cozy little place called Fruit of the Spirit, and Chris volunteered there from time to time, passing out schedules as people walked in or helping to prepare snacks for the Sunday school kids. Charlotte wasn't as much of a church-goer as Chris was, but she did come with him occasionally. It was on one of the days when Chris was alone that Nick approached him after service.

"Hey, Chris! I was wondering if you wanted to head over to the range. You've been here for almost two years already and I haven't even taken the time to give you some tips! You might need them during the training test." Nick winked.

"Sounds good! The range on Grovewood street, right?" Chris tucked his hands into his pockets. The murmurs of the congregation echoed from the high, peaked ceiling.

"Yup. I'll meet you out front."

"See you there."

Chris headed home to pick up his pistol. It had been a gift from his dad when Chris first received his acceptance letter from Foxglove. He put the pistol in its case and stuck it in his backpack.

The gun range sat near the southeast edge of Spectral Lakes that skirted Lake Lullaby. The entrance was a small firearms shop decked in American flags, its doors flanked by chainsaw-carved statues of bears.

Chris had been in shops like these many times with his dad. He still vividly remembered the unusually stern look on his dad's face when he'd lectured the young Chris on gun safety.

"If you ever put your finger on the trigger without intent to fire, you're breaking the rules. Never, *ever* point the barrel at anyone, even if the chamber is empty. You need to respect it, but not be afraid of it. Remember when I first taught you to ride? It's like that. Respect the horse, don't fear it."

Over the next hour, Chris and Nick shot at the provided targets, practiced their aim, and between rounds removed their thick headsets to talk to one another. Nick did his best to give some advice, but was pleasantly surprised to see how much Chris already knew. An unspoken competition ignited between them, and soon they were comparing headshot accuracy and numbers. They then took a break to munch on a few snacks from the nearby vending machine.

"You don't have to answer this if it's a tough question," Chris asked between chips, "but have you ever had to fire your gun in the field?"

Nick cocked his head to one side and peeled back the wrapping on his granola bar. "Once."

Chris leaned over the picnic table. "Really?"

"Yeah." Nick swallowed. "I was less than a year into my job at the time. A few months before I met you, I think. I was called in by the park rangers at Crowgold. They were investigating a series of thefts and wanted help from SLPD."

"What was stolen?"

"I was getting to that. Basically, over the previous few weeks, items had been going missing from campers' tents and even motorhomes. Food, supplies, that kind of thing. At first, they blamed bears, but then money and other valuables were taken. The last straw was when the pet dogs of two separate campers disappeared on the same day. Their leashes were cut and everything."

"Damn."

"Yeah, the campers' kids were in tears when I got there. Can't say I blame them. One of the rangers and I went out to investigate. Animals were ruled out pretty quickly; no claw or teeth marks, no tracks. The leash cuts were clean, as if by a knife. Anyway, the ranger helping me out was called to check on a littering issue nearby, so I continued alone for a bit. That's when someone stepped out of the woods and stared at me."

Chris's eyes were wide. "The thief returning to the scene?" he whispered.

"Calm down, Agatha Christie. I'm getting to it. She was this... strange-looking pre-teen with tangled, messy hair and ill-fitting clothes. I introduced myself and asked her name. She walked up to me and told me she'd seen the thief and his den. She said it was a man who'd scared her so much that she'd run off into the woods and hid. She'd been out there all day."

"Damn."

"Damn is right. So y'know, I asked about her parents and whether I needed to contact them, but she shook her head and said that she normally hiked alone with her dog to protect her. She hadn't seen the dog since running away from the man. I couldn't get her to tell me her parents' contact information—she was too excited. Even insisted on showing me where she'd seen the thief.

"Well, it was a bit of a walk to the site, so I asked her a few questions while she led me. She described him as best as she could—bald, middle-aged, tall. She seemed to become more relaxed as she talked, and started telling me random thoughts that came into her head. She chatted about her favorite hiking paths and the views on Mount Faraday, the way she would play with her dog—Ebony—in the rivers, and how she and Ebony would explore caves. Her face fell when she admitted that she was scared for the animal.

"I started to become a bit fond of her. She reminded me of my cousin in that endearingly talkative way. I promised her I'd do everything I could to find Ebony and the other dogs."

"*Endearingly talkative*... I get what you mean. Sounds just like Clara," Chris said with a warm smile.

Nick nodded. "Finally, we found our way to the end of the trail. She led me off the path a ways and pointed out the entrance to a cave just big enough for me to stand in. I told her to stay back while I peered inside. I couldn't see anything save for a discarded twenty-dollar bill near a bend in the tunnel. I radioed the park ranger my coordinates and asked him to come over as soon as he could. The girl and I waited in a patch of brush near the cave. I kept one eye on her and the other on the cave.

"She looked pouty—bored, even. She asked why I wasn't going in, so I had to explain that if the man was in there, it might not be safe without backup. She started to cry for her dog. Loudly. If there'd been anyone it that cave they probably would have heard it. I tried to shush her but the tears were relentless. Finally, I told her I'd take just a peek inside." Nick rolled his eyes. "Of course, she cheered up immediately."

Chris grinned. "Kids, eh?"

"So I carefully crept into the cave, my hand on my taser. Holding in a breath, I peered around the corner—and oh man, there was a veritable treasure trove of stolen items. Clothes, canned food, sleeping bags, portable heaters, the works. And, despite the darkness, I was just able to make out a small shape curled up on a pile of pillows. It was the corpse of a black Doberman. My heart sunk.

"Then I felt a set of small hands pushing into my back. I turned around to see the girl there. Her hair was even wilder, and her eyes had this glossy glare to them. Before I could get her out, she screamed at me. She said, 'Take him, Ebony! Take him!' I don't think I'll ever forget that.

"It was so dark in there I could barely make it out, but from deeper within the cave there was this dark shape— some kind of black bear. Its beady eyes glared right at us. I took the girl's arm in one hand, my pistol in the other, and slowly backed away. The girl wasn't having it. She tried to rip the gun from my grasp and push me forward at the same time. I was too big for her to push, but I was so confused and terrified that...

well, she managed to wrench the gun away from me. After, I should add, she dug her teeth into my fingers.

"'Ebony! I brought him! Hurry!' she said.

"She tried to aim the gun at me. She'd almost pulled the trigger when I snatched it back. The bear was approaching slowly now, its black nose sniffing the air. I grabbed the girl's arm tighter and backed us both around the corner. At the sound of her scream, the bear lunged—it was fast for such a giant—and pinned me under its paws. It was a mess of fur and rot, with these huge black teeth. I could barely aim straight, but I fired and a bullet pierced the thing. It let me go long enough for me to scramble to my feet and drag the girl out of the cave.

"It's admittedly a terrible idea to try to run from a bear, but I wasn't in the best state of mind. I kept going until I ran into the park ranger and told him in a flurry of words what had happened. The girl was thrashing and biting at my side. The ranger and I managed to get her under control. Thankfully, the bear wasn't following."

Chris gaped. "What was with the girl?!"

Nick sighed. "It was the ghost of her dog that made her do it, she said. A demon. It was horrible. Her entire demeanor changed. The way she spoke about the dog was unnerving. It was like all that supernatural gunk the tourist traps keep crooning about had twisted her mind.

"At first, I thought it was the trauma—but then she told me her demon dog had ordered her to kill it so it could be free. She was the one who'd murdered the damn pup. She'd been living in the woods off of all the stuff she'd stolen. Poor girl just wasn't right in the head. Turns out she'd run from her parents in Wenatchee a few months before and had been traveling through the woods with her dog ever since. Sad stuff. As far as I know, she's still in the mental hospital. As for the bear, well, we never found it. Not a body nor a blood trail."

"You sure it was a bear?"

"What else could it have been?"

"A demon dog?" Chris tried to keep a straight face.

Nick shook his head, frowning. "Girl was demented, man. Demented."

"But for real," Chris said, "I'm sorry you had to go through that. Sounds scary as hell. Thanks for telling me, though. What an experience."

"Yeah, can't say that my sense of trust wasn't shaken after that. Maybe I can't read people as well as I thought."

"Does that mean you don't trust me?" Chris pouted.

Nick rolled his eyes. "Nah, I know a sucker when I see one. You're as transparent as they come, Faraday."

"Should I be insulted?"

"Maybe."

The boys chuckled and threw away their snack wrappers. They continued shooting for another hour, but Nick wasn't as competitive as he'd been before. Sometimes Chris would catch him staring into space before blinking and regaining his composure. He said nothing. Sometimes silence was the best comfort one could give.

"What do you enjoy most about living here, huh?"

Charlotte asked, lying back on the thick picnic blanket, her eyes on the sinking sun behind the tree-laden mountains. The orange light emblazoned across the horizon bathed her in its glow, reminding Chris of the first day they'd met. She rubbed her legs, which, she'd said, were sore from all the ballet practice.

Chris dipped his bare feet in the water and munched on a cheese-covered cracker.

"I just really like the outdoors," he said at last. "Honestly, it was hard choosing between being an officer or a park ranger. I still think about doing ranger duty instead sometimes." He brushed his hand against the pine tree he was leaning against. "That and the town really has its own personality. I love small places like this—isolated little worlds with their own interconnected relationships and cultures. Besides," he said, watching a crow take off from the tree above him and fly toward the sunset, "I feel like I'm connected to this place. Like my ancestors brought me back. Sounds stupid but it's true."

Charlotte's eyes fell. "Yeah... I understand. Trust me."

The two sat in silence, breathing in the crisp air and listening to the calls of distant ducks landing on the water. Several boats slid among them, kids on board throwing bread crusts to the birds beneath.

"I guess that's the reason I want to get out of here," Charlotte mused.

Chris looked at her. "What do you mean?"

"I want to go to Paris. As soon as I can. Open a ballet studio. Rent a cute little apartment overlooking the Seine. Sing songs while walking through the *Champ de Mars*. Leave everything behind." She turned to face him, her eyes burning. "Except you."

Chris leaned in next to her and wrapped her hand in his. He could feel her warmth spreading through his body.

"I'll come with you."

Her expression melted into concern. "But you love this place. And the officer job..." She sighed. "I don't want my impossible dream to ruin yours, Chris."

Chris held her tighter. *Should I do it now? Is now the right time? God help me.*

"Wherever you go, I'll follow."

And he meant it. So much so that he pulled out a CD case from his bag and handed it to her.

"What on earth is this? Are we in the early 2000s or something?" She laughed and examined the cover. "Oh—oh my God." It was a *Best of Vincent Firestar* album, complete with a picture of the star in all his scowling, red-headed glory. "My love of screamo was supposed to be a *secret*. Did you snoop on my phone?"

Chris shook his head. "Your earbuds are loud. Now come on, open it."

"Chris, I swear if this is some cheesy way of asking me to marry you..." She stared at the open case—or, more specifically, at the jeweled ring tucked where the CD should have been. "Damnit. It is!" Her face lit up.

For the first time since Chris had met her, Charlotte was lost for words. Her eyes welled up, and a smile so pure and happy that Chris lost his breath for a moment spread across her cheeks. Time stood still as, gently, she pulled him into a kiss. The last vestiges of sunset washed over them like a blanket being drawn back.

"I'm assuming that's a yes?" Chris asked with a smirk.

Charlotte handled most of the wedding planning, to Chris's relief. It was a humble little ceremony that took place in a beautiful vista on Faraday Mountain. Chris's close family and friends attended, including Nick and his wife Faye.

The moment "I do"s were said, the very mountain seemed to shift. Something was in the air; wind buffeted their skin as if prodding them forward or pulling them away. Crows cawed. The lake's water pounded the shore.

Then, all at once, the world was still.

Chapter 4
Dance of the Swan

With final semester exams looming, Chris and Charlotte hadn't had much time for hiking or lazing by the lake. Charlotte had been teaching ballet to older kids, and her mentor signed her up for a big competition in Seattle, a show that could make or break her dance career. All the big agencies would be represented, critics watching with judging eyes—and so, she practiced her heart out every single day, normally coming home at night with sore feet and a hopeful heart.

Meanwhile, Chris was due to begin his three-month police training program. He was wickedly excited for it and spent most days either studying, working out, or at the range. Sometimes, he took calorie-burning runs around Lake Lullaby, the smallest of the town's three surrounding lakes.

During those rare free evenings, he'd

carve mini statuettes and decorations for his and Charlotte's new home, a small rental cabin in the woods on the outskirts of town near Foxglove. Charlotte had taken over as "interior decorator," working her magic with thrift store-bought furniture and refurbished drapery.

They'd made sure, whenever possible, to set aside money for Paris. It was going to take time to earn the funds but, thanks to their jobs and a couple of scholarships, the dream didn't seem as far off as they'd thought. Chris had carved a little wooden Eiffel Tower for the mantelpiece to remind them of their goal.

Chris still played games online with his *Valkyrie* friends and made music, but

those things were becoming harder and harder to find time for with so much of *life* getting in the way. But, despite this, Chris felt *happy*. He didn't quite know what life had in store for him, but he was eager to find out. And, whenever he felt doubt, he prayed, asking for direction.

Finally, Charlotte's big day arrived. She rose in the wee hours of the morning and began readying herself—stretching, practicing, getting everything in order. By the time Chris had dragged himself out of bed, she was fully decked out in her rented Swan Princess costume, a set of white wings wrapped around her waist and her collar swathed in feathers. She carefully placed her satin ballet shoes in her blue bag and turned to face Chris, a nervous but proud smile on her face.

"This is the start of it, Chris," she said breathlessly. "I couldn't have done it without you."

Chris pulled her in for a kiss.

The theatre was full of people. Audience members quietly chatted among themselves, the panel of judges organized their rating forms, and agents typed notes into their tablets.

Chris's stomach knotted. *I do* not *envy how she must be feeling right now.*

The lights dimmed and, all at once, the orchestra burst into life.

For the next half an hour, dancers, performing one by one, showed off their talents. The audience applauded after each performance, and Chris nervously glanced at the judges to gauge their reactions.

And then, the curtains parted. A lone figure stood, her pale arms raised to the sky. The orchestra swelled, the opening strain of "Swan's Theme" from Tchaikovsky's *Swan Lake* filling the auditorium. Charlotte, as Odette, lunged, her body languid, controlled, her movements relaxed and loose—and the magic took hold, her body twisting, hardening, her arms fluttering. Her movements slowed as she was overtaken by grief—for the sorcery had taken her, cursing her to remain a swan by day and a human only by night on the waters of the enchanted lake.

Chris had seen *Swan Lake* before and, as such, recalled the story as Charlotte danced through a condensed version of the tale. A prince begged by his mother to soon marry hunts in the forest, whereupon he comes across Odette as a swan and sees her transform into a human. They fall in love, but all is cut short when dawn arrives and Odette must once again become a swan. Later, at a costumed royal ball, the evil wizard Rothbart, who cursed Odette in the first place, attends, his daughter disguised as Odette. The prince dances with her and, at the end of the night, declares his intention to marry her. The true Odette watches the scene from the window, and is so distraught she flees to the lake. Once the deception is revealed, the heartbroken prince rushes into the woods to find Odette. Though she forgives him, her heart is forever shattered, and she cannot bear to live any longer as a swan. The ballet ends with both Odette and the prince sinking into the lake, their arms intertwined as their souls ascend to heaven.

Though Charlotte was alone on stage, she masterfully told the sad tale through her movements; every turn was purposeful, every step perfectly aligned. She bounded and twirled across the stage, leaving Chris breathless.

Suddenly, she stopped, her eyes caught on something in the audience. There was a moment of strange stillness before her body jerked, falling again into step. Confused, Chris turned, scanning the crowd. Whatever she'd seen, it had affected her; even now, her face was red, her brows furrowed, her movements hard and sharp. Betrayed by the prince, Charlotte's Odette jabbed and kicked, ran across the stage, and collapsed to the ground, succumbing to silent sobs.

An audience member could have interpreted this as all part of the show—Charlotte just another ballerina who slathered her performance in dramatic, rich emotion—but Chris knew better. Something was very wrong.

Chris watched, frowning, as Charlotte spun low, unable to bear her curse any longer, and drowned in the lake. Without a prince, Charlotte's rendition of the death seemed quieter, lonelier than normal. The stage swam with blue light, Odette sinking ever deeper before her last breath left her body. The music faded.

There was a silence.

As one, the audience erupted into applause. After a moment, Chris joined in, his mind racing. Charlotte's face was hard, any individual emotion hard to make out.

It took all of Chris's willpower to stay in his seat as the rest of the dancers performed. Finally, as the last dancer bowed and left the stage, the judges rose and disappeared to deliberate. Pushing through the shifting audience as they filed into the lobby, Chris bolted backstage. He found Charlotte sat in front of a mirror framed by light bulbs, her hair unpinned, a long strand covering one eye. She combed it through over and over, her gaze impossibly distant.

"Charlotte? Hey, are you all right? What's wrong?" Chris touched her shoulder, jerking back when she jumped, whipping around to face him.

Her gaze was sharp but softened immediately. "Oh, Chris!" She cupped his hand in hers. Her skin was clammy. "I'm sorry. You surprised me."

Chris's brows knitted. "Did something happen during the show? You looked like you'd seen the Lady or something. I was... really concerned." He brushed the strand of hair away from her eyes, tucking it behind an ear. Charlotte dipped her head, the hair falling back over her face.

"No, nothing like that." She grasped her bottle of water and took a few gulps. "I just twisted my leg the wrong way and was angry I messed up."

"Oh," Chris responded. He felt a slow twist in his stomach. She sounded a bit off. *Is she... lying to me?*

"Sorry, Chris, I need to get ready for the judge's announcement. I'll see you afterward, okay?" She shot him a small smile before turning back to the mirror.

"All right... see you." Chris backed away, his chest tight.

Back in his seat, Chris watched the crowd as they filed back into the theater, searching for anyone he recognized. Person after person pushed past the doors and down the aisles, but Chris knew none of them. He let out a sigh and nervously adjusted his jacket.

The judges paraded onto the stage followed by the young dancers that had performed that night. Their costumes glittered beneath the stage lights in patterns of pastel hues.

Charlotte seemed to be completely composed. She stared into space, focusing on anything but the audience.

Chris dug his nails into his hands as the judges announced award-winners in particular categories. Minutes ticked by, elderly voices announcing name after name, until, finally, a crow-looking woman dressed in black glanced down at a notecard in her satin-gloved hands.

"And for Best Storytelling, the award goes to... Charlotte Ramsey!"

The crowd applauded. Chris stood up and clapped, his beaming grin finally bringing Charlotte's attention to the crowd. Her posture broke for a moment, her eyes welling up as a smile broke through. The crow-woman placed a simple medal around her neck and handed her a check.

This is it. Chris thought, his chest swelling. *This is the start of it all.*

Chapter 5
Swan Song

After the show, Charlotte talked with several interested agents for an hour or so. They exchanged email addresses, chatted about her career goals, and several agents offered her their services over glasses of wine at the theatre bar. Chris didn't talk much; instead, he watched Charlotte's face light up the more excited she got.

Finally, Chris drove a thoroughly exhausted Charlotte and her ballet bag full of business cards back home. She looked about ready to collapse but, as she turned the handle to their cabin, she turned to face Chris, her lips pursed.

"Hey, what's that?" She pointed to a small wrapped package on one of the wooden lawn chairs near the lake's edge. The shiny wrapping paper caught in the moon's beams.

"Ah, that," Chris replied with a small smile. "It was meant to be a gift for you because of how hard you've been working, but, since you're so tired right now, maybe we could open it tomorr—"

"Chris, come on, you shouldn't have!" Charlotte said, making a beeline for the gift. She picked it up and sank into the lawn chair. Chris sat in the one beside her.

"All right, then, if you insist!" Chris said with a smirk.

The gift was unwrapped in an instant, revealing a carved wooden swan, its chipped edges catching the light. Charlotte slowly examined the trinket, her hands trembling.

"Woah, hey, hey, are you all right?" Chris leaned over, his arm wrapping around her shoulder.

Charlotte bent over the swan, her body wracked with sobs.

Chris blinked, his mouth dry. "Charlotte, hey, talk to me! What's gotten you so riled up tonight?"

She shook her head, cradling the swan in her arms. Finally, she looked up at Chris. Her skin sparkled—glittering makeup mixed with tears.

"I don't know what I'd do without you, Christopher Faraday," she stated, the corners of her mouth dimpling. "I just don't know what I'd do." She shook her head before leaning into his chest, burying her face in his suit jacket.

A thousand thoughts flew around Chris's mixed-up brain. *What did she lie about? Why is she getting so emotional right now? Is she on her period? Is that how it works? Jesus, what am I even thinking? Is she not telling me something? Or did my stupid little swan really mean that much to her? Is my craftsmanship good enough to bring women to tears? Did I accidentally spill garlic powder on the wrapping paper?*

Of course, every echoing voice silenced when Charlotte slid her hand down to his belt and moved her lips to his neck.

Oh. Well, then.

They embraced one another, kissing softly, but the cold wind rising from the lake cut through Chris's suit and chilled him to the bone. Fog wove between the trees, spilling into a tapestry of mist on the lake's surface.

"Should we take this inside?" Chris asked. Something about the lake felt familiar tonight—and not in a good way.

He could tell Charlotte sensed it too. However, instead of looking out at the lake, she turned her gaze toward the dark woods. She frowned.

"What is *that*?" she asked, nervously tugging at her almost completely undone hair. She pointed to a hulking shape between the pines past their cabin. It wasn't a person, but rather...

Chris squinted in the moonlight. "Is that a *house*?"

He rose on unsteady feet and, after fetching a flashlight from the cabin, approached the shaded tree line. Charlotte was immediately at his side.

A way away, tucked between bushes and patches of white lilies, was a painted lady; a small Victorian home. It looked ancient—partially dilapidated, its exterior coated in dirt and vines. More white lilies poked through missing tiles on the roof.

"Where the hell did *that* come from?" Chris cried.

Charlotte's mouth was agape, her eyes squinted. "How is that possible? I—what?"

The flashlight bathed the house in a stark white. Charlotte gripped Chris's free hand tightly.

He gazed at the rotten, broken floorboards of the porch and, above, the chipped, faded paint on the walls. The foundation appeared as if had been slowly sinking into the soft dirt.

"I mean—it looks like it's been here for a hell of a long time," Chris said. He shone his light through the upstairs window, but saw nothing but darkness.

"This is insane." Charlotte put a hand over her mouth. "How on earth have we not seen this before?"

"I've walked this path hundreds of times..." It felt like a snake was slithering up his spine.

Charlotte took out her phone and snapped a few pictures of the house before turning to Chris. "Should I call someone?" she said, her voice trembling, "the cops?"

"I don't know. Maybe Nick's cell. He should see this."

The flashlight beam caught a first-floor

window. A blur of color from inside set the hairs on Chris's arms on end. He slowly approached, sweat beading on his brow.

A sitting room appeared before him. Through the dusty, cobwebbed glass, he saw Victorian lounge chairs and side-tables. Dusty photos lined the walls and an oaken cabinet sat next to a cinder-filled fireplace.

But none of this held Chris's attention. Rather, his widening eyes stared at the blood-soaked body of a woman on the ground, her limbs severed from her torso. Next to her, a suited man lay, clutching a golden pocket watch in his white-gloved hand. His head rested a few feet away. It looked as if someone had tried to saw through his legs—blood seeped from raw, gaping wounds, white flesh hanging in fish-like chunks.

A terrified scream escaped from Chris's lips. A flock of ebony crows burst from the roof, cawing and shrieking as they disappeared into the sky.

Charlotte peeked over his shoulder and gasped, gagging too much to even cry out. She grasped Chris's arm, her nails digging into his skin.

"Call the cops! Now!" Chris managed to croak, stumbling back and weakly pushing Charlotte toward their car. "We need to go!"

With a trembling hand, Charlotte dialed. She let go of Chris and stood still, her eyes blanched.

"Charlotte?"

Chris whirled around, reaching for her. He stopped.

A large black hand was wrapped around Charlotte's shoulder. It almost looked to be made of shadows; writhing shapes slithered and moved beneath the skin. Chris opened his mouth, but no sound emerged. A huge figure towered behind Charlotte. Red eyes bored into Chris, their depth astounding, as if they were bullet holes shot through his head that went on forever.

"No," screamed Charlotte, "*no! Why are you here? Leave me alone!*" She dropped her phone, clawing at her face. She didn't even look behind her.

Before Chris could move, the shadow raised a wicked-looking ax and, with one savage jerk, sunk it deep into Charlotte's abdomen.

Chris's heart stopped.

Gore burst from the wound as the ax was ripped away. Charlotte fell to her knees, her face white, blood bubbling from her lips.

A terrible scream ripped through Chris's throat. Adrenaline shot through his body and, more quickly than he'd ever moved before, he swept Charlotte into his arms and sprinted for the car. Her eyes were empty, her words choking.

"Chris—!"

"*Hey!* Hey! It's going to be okay!" Chris murmured, his eyes glazed, the world swimming around him.

Charlotte's fingers were splayed over her slick abdomen, trying in vain to keep herself together. Strangled moans leaked from her open mouth. Chris glanced back. The shadow hadn't moved. The ax gleamed in its hand.

"L—listen," Chris stuttered, "I'm gonna keep you safe, okay?" He pressed his cheek into Charlotte's hair, now wet with tears. "Just—"

A wet whistling sound rang in Chris's ear as he reached the lake's shore, and pain exploded in his back, sending him crashing to the ground. Charlotte rolled out of his grasp, stretched out on the sand. Blood squeezed between her fingers.

Helpless, face coated in gravel, Chris stared at Charlotte, their eyes locking. He tried to reach for her hand, tried to move his lips, but was paralyzed. Darkness began to creep from the edges of his vision, and he tried to blink it back, sharp wheezes escaping his lips and warm blood soaking his back.

The shadow stood over Chris. It cocked its head, its red eyes examining him. At last, it reached for the ax embedded in his back and pulled it out. Chris's body violently shuddered in response.

The husband and wife locked eyes, their bodies illuminated in scarlet light. Charlotte's face contorted. She'd pulled her legs up to her chest, torn pieces of her ballet stockings fluttering in the wind.

"Chris, no!" she wept. "Chris!" Her chin trembled. "We never... we never escaped..." She grasped at her face with her hands, smearing blood across her cheeks. "I'll always... be trapped here." She let out a low moan, the sound rising into a weak wail.

Black shapes like little rats crawled along the shadow's body. Oozing ebony veins pulsed in its neck. It raised the gore-soaked ax above its head.

Charlotte's brown eyes swiveled to meet Chris's. "Chris, I—I'm sorry," she whispered. "I... I'm..." She took a stuttering breath. "I never deserved you."

Chris desperately tried to move, to speak. Darkness drowned his mind.

"I love you, Christopher Faraday." Charlotte grasped his hand in hers.

The moon was a white pearl in the sky, ripe and shining in its glory. A breeze played with Charlotte's pale hair, brushing it into the water. All the birds of the night were silent, as if their breath had been knocked from them in tandem with Chris's. The shape of a falling ax reflected in Charlotte's deep brown irises.

The last thing Chris saw as his eyes rolled

back was a singular wooden swan floating on the lake's surface, drifting ever farther away.

Chapter 6
White Lilies

Empty.

Black water—

filling his lungs,

seeping into his veins.

So cold.

Oh! There—the shore. Black sand.

He pulls himself out.

Why are his hands covered in blood?

Oh, she put it there.

Wait. Look.

There she is.

She's standing on a black island.

But... black water is flooding it.

She won't escape, will she?

She is angry. Red.

But she sees him. She is white.

She is afraid. So afraid.

He reaches out, but she is too far.

He cannot leave; black sand forms walls.

Why? Why can't he go back to the water?

It's up to her knees.

Her shape contorts. Feathers erupt.

She has wings. Can she fly?

No. Too late.

They're soaked, too heavy to fly.

She cries black tears.

A single white lily grows out of her mouth.

As water rises, it withers.

She turns, walks into the deep.

He screams for her.

Asks her to come back.

She goes on, under the water,

Everything still.

A black pane of glass.

It has swallowed her.

She never escaped

it.

Silence.

Everything is

silent.

Unbearable.

Alone.

Oh.

There is a voice now.

A different voice. She says:

"Christopher!"

He looks down.

A woman—she moves

as if through air.

She looks familiar.

"Christopher."

…

"You have a job to do, Faraday."

Chapter 7

Missing Piece

Chris's eyes slowly rolled open. The light was soft and gray—a curtain had been pulled over the far window. Everything was muted, muffled somehow; it was as if his brain were submerged in syrup. There was a peculiar tightness around his chest and a dull throbbing echoed from his back. His fingers twitched and, when he looked down, he found an IV hooked up to his arm. A mask was strapped over his nose and mouth.

Hmm?

His eyes rolled toward the window, and bursts of color entered his vision. Hundreds of flowers were bundled and stacked neatly on the windowsill and floor beside him, some tied with ribbons and decked in shiny paper, fat teddy bears with *Get well soon!* on their plush bellies strewn among them. Many of the names attached to the cards were those of the church congregation.

Chris felt chills run through his body. There was something heavy in the pit of his stomach—something rising. It took him a moment to realize it was dread.

His head lolled to the left. A woman in nurse's garb peered down at him, giving him a gentle smile and a wave. She said a few words, though Chris had trouble putting meaning to them.

"How are you feeling?" she said again.

"Huh?" he murmured. "What's going on?"

The nurse was checking his vitals, her hands working diligently. She slowed to respond to him. "You've been through intensive surgery, Mr. Faraday. Your back suffered a major laceration and two of your ribs were broken. This led to a minor pneumothorax—a collapsed lung." Her voice softened and she clasped her hands together. "Thankfully, you're no longer in any danger and should make a full recovery."

Chris blinked several times. "How—?" A lump formed in his throat and he coughed violently.

"It's all right, Mr. Faraday. Breath slowly. How are you feeling?"

He shivered. "Cold."

The nurse nodded. "You'll have the chills for about an hour. Anesthesia symptoms. They'll wear off soon." She wrote several scribbled notes on a clipboard and flashed him another smile. "You may also be experiencing confusion, slight memory loss, an upset stomach—"

There was a knock at the door.

"Excuse me for a moment."

The nurse opened the door, and Chris spotted a man in uniform.

Nick! That's Nick! Pieces started coming together. Everything still felt disgustingly foggy, but Chris could see the outlines of recent memories, their details slowly crystallizing.

His heart pounded. His fingers trembled. He became more aware of the pain radiating from his back. A single word bubbled to his lips.

"*Charlotte!*"

It was as if a hot brand had seared her face into his eyes. He saw her before him, her form like white fire stained red. Her mouth was open, her face contorted in a scream.

"Charlotte!" Chris cried louder, his head beaded with sweat as he rose from the pillow.

The nurse returned, a man with a pen in his hand with her. They hovered over Chris, glancing worriedly at his heart rate monitor.

"Are you all right, Mr. Faraday?" asked the female nurse.

"Did you need something?" asked the man, clicking his pen nervously.

"Where is Charlotte?" Chris choked out, his eyes bloodshot. He tried to rise into a sitting position, but pain rocketed through his chest. The hands of the nurses gently pushed him down.

"No, keep lying down. You need your rest!"

Chris's hands clenched and unclenched, his wild stare flitting between random spots. Black shapes seeped from the corners of the room, their masses bulging like fungi from a tree trunk. Red eyes like bullet holes drilled into every shape, all closing in on him. Chris screamed and rolled off the bed, staggering to his feet and ca-reening into a collection of bouquets.

"Mr. Faraday! Calm down! You'll hurt

yourself!"

The nurses moved toward him with pleading hands, but their necks snapped back in tandem, their eyes melting from their skulls, leaving nothing but red.

Several vases shattered as Chris stumbled back. The various tubes jutting from him went taut. He snatched up a piece of broken vase and thrust it toward the nurses.

"Tell me what you did with Charlotte!" Chris cried.

The nurses growled, dead lips flapping, and stepped back. One reached for a red button on the side of the bed. The other moved to the door.

Chris floundered. The black shadows were moving closer, and he slashed, shrieking garbled questions, but they just kept coming. They seeped into his glass-cut legs, slithered into his wrists, and blackened the edges of his vision.

Nick burst into the room. He called out, but his voice came from somewhere deep beneath the earth.

With a final moan, Chris fell to his knees.

Nick, murmuring soothing nothings, gently eased the glass from Chris's limp hand. He led him back toward the bed, sitting with him.

"Chris?" he said, his voice slow and alien. "Chris?"

Head drooping low, Chris slumped forward. Silently, a nurse pressed a button, and liquid flowed through one of the IV tubes still attached.

"Where is Charlotte...?" he mumbled, his voice cracking. His bleeding hands trembled in his lap.

Nick went stiff. "We're doing everything we can to solve this, Chris," he said at last.

"Where is she?"

"We've been examining the scene and collecting evidence—"

"*Where is she?*"

With a shaking hand, Nick removed his hat and held it to his heart.

That was all it took. Chris gasped for breath. His whole body thundered with his erratic heartbeat.

Charlotte—sinking into black water.

Screaming, bleeding, fading...

Sucking in a shaking breath, he raised his hands to his face. He stared blankly between bloody fingers.

Nick tentatively put his hand on Chris's shoulder.

"I'm so sorry..." He rubbed his tired eyes. "God, I'm so sorry, Chris..."

Chris sank back. Whatever the nurse had put into him had started its work. Blackness, cool and quiet, washed over him. His breaths softening, he fell into it, letting oblivion ease his pain.

Chapter 8
Aftermath

The next few months were hell on Earth for Christopher Faraday.

After his violent outburst, he'd been cuffed to his bed. He was kept there for what felt like weeks—his doctors said they had to wait for the fresh wounds on his hands to heal. As soon as he felt well enough, he was interrogated by the police. It was torture trying to explain the details of what he'd seen; the cops just stared at him blankly when he spoke of the shadow man or the Victorian house, and he caught them on more than one occasion shooting one another incredulous looks. He'd been informed that no such house was found anywhere in the vicinity.

So, of course, he'd been given psychological evaluations by three separate psychologists, and finally ended up being transferred to a mental hospital.

His parents visited whenever possible. As soon as they'd heard of the incident, they rushed to Washington. They comforted their son as best they could and tried desperately to convince him to move back to Texas with them, but he refused.

The investigation went on, shaking the town of Spectral Lakes to its core. People talked about it constantly; there hadn't been such a horrific murder in the town's history for decades.

According to the papers and nosy internet tabloids, late on Saturday night, September 28, a 911 call had been dialed by Charlotte Fenella Faraday. She'd not responded to the operator's questions—instead, a series of screams and panicked cries were heard. Officers and an ambulance were dispatched to the location but, by the time they arrived, it was too late.

Christopher Korbin Faraday had been found unconscious, floating face-up on the surface of Lake Spectral, his back severely lacerated and his body covered in bruises. Charlotte had initially been missing but, after Christopher had been taken to hospital, officers found Charlotte's severed arms and legs on her bed in the couple's home. Her torso and head had not yet been found.

No significant DNA evidence was recovered. Some physical evidence indicated the murderer was a person of very large stature, but others, like footprints, indicated someone smaller. The police left open the possibility of two killers, though it didn't match up with the witness testimony.

Speaking of the witness testimony, Christopher Faraday's account of phantom houses and a murderer made of shadows confused detectives to no end. Blood samples from that night proved that neither he nor Charlotte were drunk or under the influence of drugs. Officials argued over whether his word was even viable in court, arguing insanity—but mental health experts had examined Chris and almost unanimously determined that he wasn't suffering from psychosis, schizophrenia, or any other hallucinatory disorder. All they could say for sure was that he had severe post-traumatic stress disorder.

Even so, some folks thought Chris was just a poor, sad man whose brain had made up the whole thing to save his sanity. Others thought he was straight-up insane. Yet some found him entirely suspicious and wondered if he'd made up the story to cover for the *real* murderer—a seedy hitman he'd hired to do the dirty deed. Only a rare few believed him, mostly kooks and those who, for one reason or another, were invested in the lake's supernatural legends.

Eventually, the case went completely cold. What was found of Charlotte's remains were buried in the Spectral Lakes Cemetery, and a memorial for her was set up near the spot she'd died. The Faraday's cabin home was torn down, since Chris had moved into an apartment in town instead, and no one wanted to rent the place where Charlotte Faraday's limbs had been found.

Christopher quit college, all of his once-palpable passion gone. He was like a ghost around town, drifting from one place to the next, hardly ever seen. He lived off of his savings and the money his parents continued to send him. The less he was heard from, the more rumors grew. Young teens gossiped about spotting him sitting at the lake's edge, a ukulele in-hand that he never played a single note on. Middle-aged mothers chatted back and forth about the tired bags that now hung under his eyes, his uncombed mess of hair, and the stubble he didn't bother to shave. Schoolchildren stopped and stared on their way home when they saw him leaning against a pine tree and staring out at the sunset, a block of wood in his hands that he would hack at, carving random, meaningless patterns until it was nothing but chips.

"That Chris Faraday, I tell ya..." said a sun-tanned grandpa to his chess partner one summer afternoon. "That's a shell of a man if I've ever seen one."

"So young, too. God, what a shame."

"Mmhmm. Unholy things going on with that whole case, I predict. Been praying for him."

"Unholy things? Frank, do you believe the boy's story?"

"I do. I've seen a hell of a lotta things in my time, *especially* on these lakes."

"Really, now?"

"I'd bet my Chrysler DeSoto on it."

"Damn, you must be serious then."

"Yessir. And I don't have one doubt in my mind that one of these days, Christopher is gonna poke his nose in spiritual matters he ain't prepared to face."

"Like what? Demons?"

"Worse. Old, dead, mean *women*."

Chapter 9
Of Sirens and Crosses

There were too many crows up in the trees. Not an unusual amount, mind you, but enough to make Chris feel uncomfortable. Then again, he never felt entirely comfortable these days. There was always a slight shake to his hands; a jerk to his walk. He'd start like a skittish doe at nothing, especially when the elder pines of Spectral Lakes closed around him like ancient bark walls.

Yet, despite the almost overwhelming feeling of shiny black eyes watching his every move and branches closing in over his head, he walked on. Twigs cracked under his black boots, the noise thunderous against the silence. A few of the crows shuffled, hopping from one foot to the other as they adjusted their feathers. Chris slid a hand into his SLPD hoodie, his fingertips brushing against a smooth plastic square.

Eventually, the foliage parted to reveal a shaded clearing leading to the lake's edge. A large foundation, inside of which was a smooth patch of dirt, was all that remained of Chris's old home. The bright yellow of forgotten police tape peeked from under overgrown bushes, and the lake rippled against the rocks of the shore, the dark water almost beckoning men to soundlessly slip beneath its surface and disappear.

Chris was finding it increasingly hard to breathe. He could almost taste the black water from his nightmares. His glazed eyes scanned the woods behind him, as if he expected a shadowy figure to writhe into being at any moment.

As far as Chris knew, no one had set foot here for months, least of all him. Yet now he stood here, his gaze slowly drifting to the small wooden structure beneath the tree closest to the lodge foundation. It was almost like a doll-house—a tiny slanted wooden roof covering an open shelf. The backmost panel held a framed picture of Charlotte—a picture taken at the Spectral Lakes Fall Festival, her body wrapped in a slim light blue gown. Small newspaper clippings relating to her ballet achievements were pinned around the box, as well as cute, crudely written sympathy letters from her young students at the studio. A pair of her silk ballet shoes rested among a bed of white lilies.

A fresh stab of pain pierced Chris's heart. He focused on pulling out the plastic square in his pocket. It was the CD case for the *Best of Vincent Firestar*. With trembling hands, he set it upright against the box.

He stood for a while, his hands in his pockets and his pine-green eyes resting on the memorial. A chill wind whipped up, darkening clouds borne upon it.

The rain was naught but a drizzle at first, but it prompted Chris to do what he'd come to do. From his backpack, he removed a large blue tarp and draped it over himself and the shrine. He crouched low on the yellowing grasses, the little light that shone through enough for him to gaze at Charlotte's photo.

For over an hour, raindrops bombarded the tarp. Chris was unwilling to leave. Though the ground beneath his shoes turned to mud and

water spattered his jeans, he remained.

When the storm finally passed, Chris came out and allowed himself to stretch. He decided to leave the tarp over the memorial—just in case.

The winds still howled in his ears, and he pulled his hoodie tight around him. A few curses left his lips when his shoe hit something hard. He glanced down at whatever it was, head cocked.

"What the—"

The corner of a bronze-ish metal box stuck out of the ground, its edge revealed by the rain's erosion. Chris kicked away at the dirt around the object and, bending, yanked out the whole thing.

It wasn't a box after all; it was a metal cross embedded with three sapphires, one on each upper branch of the cross.

Where did this come from?

Chris's face scrunched up as he examined the object, turning it over in his hands and brushing off mud. There was an engraving on the back. A name.

Eleanor Heron Faraday. Chris frowned. *Faraday?*

The wind whipped by, beckoning him

toward the lake. He obliged for the moment, crouching at the shoreline to wash the cross. As the cross sank beneath the clear water, the wind quietened; it became whispery and low, and the longer Chris washed the cross, the more they seemed to form words.

Faraday... Edward...?

Chris jumped back, head whipping from side to side, eyes wide. The tremble of his hands worsened, the wet cross almost slipping from his grip.

No... not Edward...

All at once, the breeze stopped. The air in the clearing was completely still. Gently, Chris stepped back. He put the cross in his hoodie pocket.

Give... BACK!

With a wretched scream, the wind slammed into him. A writhing figure burst from the water's surface, skin torn and withered, eyes black and deep, a bony fishtail arcing from its hips. It began to crawl toward Chris, its long claws sinking into the mud.

Chris fell, a scream caught in his throat,

cold terror prickling at his skin, before scrambling away. He rose, tripped, rose again, and sprinted into the thick black tree line. His heart thundered in his chest and a familiar feeling of helplessness swiftly wormed its way into his psyche. He glanced back, the beginnings of another downpour blurring his vision.

Behind, the wretch of a creature stared at him with piercing ebony eyes. Her mouth seeped black liquid, which spattered the memorial's tarp as she whipped back, letting out a blood-curdling screech.

The last thing Chris saw of her was her shoulders slump, her chest heave—and there, around her neck, an identical metal cross. Then she was gone, leaving nothing but the gashes in the mud. Chris didn't stop—he sprinted back the way he'd come, rain soaking his hoodie and running down his tear-stained face. Sopping hair stuck to his forehead.

The only thought that reverberated within his skull was the realization that the wretch's voice was the very same he'd been hearing in his nightmares.

In a dimly lit apartment containing sparse furniture and even fewer decorations, Chris sat huddled in a large towel. He'd not bothered to eat or shower; instead, he stared, transfixed, at his computer monitor, typing variations of "Spectral Lakes Lady of the Lake Sightings" and "History of Lady of the Lake, Spectral Lakes" into his browser. The monitor's glow washed his deeply creased face in blue hues that contrasted with the red of his phone's light, which currently displayed an extensive list of paranormal-themed podcasts.

He paused for a moment, rubbing his weary eyes and giving himself a good smack on the head. Dozens of tabs and newly minted bookmarks hovered on screen, each displaying the same information over and over.

...Not much is known about Spectral Lakes' own cryptid woman...

...People who claim to have seen her report a blue figure standing on the lake...

...She's a mermaid-looking-thing! That's what I saw. A gross, rotten beast!...

...A tourist claimed to hear haunting singing and gentle whispers...

...When I was five, I had the encounter. I was climbing Mount Faraday...

...No one knows how she is summoned or where she comes from...

...Sightings are rare; most who have encountered her only see her once...

Pursing his lips, he minimized everything and pulled up a fresh window. His fingers hovered over the keys. *"Faraday Family Spectral Lakes History."* Several pertinent results popped up.

...Helped found the town. Their horses hauled lumber and stone...

...Owned a horse ranch on what is now known as Mount Faraday, a part of Crowgold National Park...

Chris's chest tightened, his foot tapping against his chair leg.

...Edward Wolfram Faraday broke tradition by virtually abandoning the horse-rancher life and becoming a missionary. He traveled the world with his wife—

Chris sucked in a breath.

—Eleanor Heron Faraday.

Shit. SHIT.

Everything was coming together. Specifically, the realization that his great-great-grandfather may have committed uxoricide. Could he have left Spectral Lakes in order to flee being arrested?

Did he drown her in the lake? Strangle her and dispose of her body in the water?

A feeling of nausea swept over Chris. He slumped into his chair and grasped the nearly empty beer can from his ring-stained desk.

My... my great-great-grandmother is the Lady of the Lake.

Memories of the *thing* that had killed Charlotte slithered into his head. The man made of shadows had looked nothing like the Lady.

No, she couldn't have done it. But if it wasn't her... well, what if she knows who did?

A fork of lightning illuminated the world

for just a moment. If someone on the street below had looked up to the window on the third floor, they would have seen a man with sopping wet hair holding a metal cross in his hands before him, a wild look in his eyes.

Chapter 10
Hunt

The tinkling of a bell announced Chris's arrival at the Spectral Lakes Souvenir and Gift Shop. It was a tiny place filled to the brim with Lady of the Lake merchandise: various postcards, key chains, branded hats, sunglasses, down jackets, sand art, outdoor magazines, tiny bottles of fool's gold flakes, locally sourced apples, and handmade woodcrafts and jewelry. It was like the entire spirit of the town had been condensed into one room, so visually busy that Chris found it hard to focus on any one thing.

"Welcome!" said a sing-song voice. A head emerged from behind a stack of folded *I Survived a Night on Spectral Lake* t-shirts. It was Veronica Shores. "How can I help you—"

A flicker of recognition sparked in her eyes when she saw him. Her excessively wide smile waned slightly.

"Ah, hello, Mr. Faraday. I don't think I've formally met you yet!" She stepped out from behind the shirt-covered desk and, with only a hint of hesitation, held out her hand for him to shake. He did so.

"I'm Veronica," she declared, pointing at the name tag pinned to her blue-green tie-dye t-shirt. "Owner and proprietor of this lil' patch o' culture!"

Chris noted the large, tacky, obviously handmade jewelry hanging from her ears and neck, her beige cargo shorts, and her almost blindingly white socks and neon blue sneakers.

"Well, I guess you know who I am," he retorted.

Veronica's smile didn't even waver. "Yup!"

A moment passed.

"May I interest you in some of our newest products? We just stocked a glow-in-the-dark Lady of the Lake dining set perfect for spooky stories by the campfire in our own Crowgold National Park!"

"Actually, I came here to ask about the Lady of the Lake."

The woman's eyes widened slightly.

"Oh! Products or information? Our full stock of Lady-related merchandise is in the labeled section here. I have a selection of informational pamphlets over here, such as *A Speculative History of the Spectral Lakes Specter*, *The Lady of the Lake Sighting Location Guide*, and *The SHOCKING Collection of Spectral Lakes Paranormal Photographs!*" She held up sun-wrinkled hands and motioned toward a nearby shelf. "And don't forget the buy-one-get-one-free offer on our 'ghostly' caramel apples! The caramel is dyed blue and we put little ghost-shaped gummies on top! Don't forget our Foxglove University line of merch! Go Foxes!"

Chris blinked several times and waited for the sales spiel to finish. As she talked, he picked up a few of the pamphlets and flipped through them.

"—And there you have it! So, what'll it be, Mr. Faraday?"

"I need to talk with someone who's seen the Lady of the Lake and knows how to find her."

"Well, as I said, we have many pamphlets and even books dealing with the topic—"

"Not paper. People. I can talk to."

"Uhm, I'm afraid we don't have people in stock at the moment—"

"I'm talking about you—wait, what?"

Veronica's mouth formed a little "o."

"Oh! I apologize. Most of my advice is product-based. I'm sort of in the zone today." She stuck a finger against her temple.

"So can you tell me what you know about her or not?" Chris's brows sunk to his eyelids.

"I'm a purveyor of wonder, culture, stories, and quality merchandise," she said, gesturing dramatically. Finally, her hands sank to her hips and her smile faded. "But I'm afraid I've never seen my dear ghostly muse in person. However, I do have a book written by my uncle that—"

"Do you know anyone I can *talk to today* that has seen her?" Chris's voice was starting to betray his growing frustration.

Veronica sighed. Her stance shifted. "I'm going to be frank with you, Mr. Faraday—"

Chris crossed his arms. *Thank God.*

"Most of the folks in this town who've seen ghosts, no matter how vividly, tend to severely question themselves for years after. They doubt their very minds, their perceptions, their thoughts and feelings. Granted, it's not uncommon for our brains to trick us, but when so many people are seeing the same things over and over, maybe there's an amount of truth to the matter. That's what I think, anyway. And, ironically, it's folks in my line of work that tend to make people think these things are nothing more than a hoax. But really, I'm just trying to get families excited about being here."

"And your point is...?"

"Not many townsfolk truly believe their encounters. But I know of one man who does. He can likely help you."

She dug a notepad and pencil from her pocket and scribbled something before ripping the page free and handing it to him.

"That's your guy."

Chris looked down at the paper (which was dotted with cute ghosts in the margins).

Jonah Adamovich

JAdamovich@FruitoftheSpiritChurch.com

"He has an email, but doesn't check it often. Today's Sunday, so you're bound to find him working at that Pentecostal church down the road. He's the tall fellow with the old-timey fashion sense and round glasses, usually tending the gardens or the graveyard if he's not handling the church budget."

An icy feeling slithered through Chris's veins. That was the church he'd attended before Charlotte's death. He'd not been back since— Charlotte was buried there.

I'll just have to grin and bear with it, he thought with a grimace. He turned to leave, so preoccupied that he forgot to thank Veronica.

He was at the door when Veronica called him.

"Say, Mr. Faraday?"

He stopped.

"About—about your testimony. I meant what I said earlier when it comes to people doubting themselves and what they've experienced. Good luck to you, whatever you're after."

Chris paused a moment. He only nodded before shutting the door behind him.

Before Charlotte's death, the Fruit of the Spirit Church had made Chris feel safe—it reminded him of the church he grew up in. But, as he stood on the steps listening to the pastor murmuring behind the wooden doors, he felt the complete opposite of comfortable. He didn't want to face his memories here—of faith, of comfort, of Charlotte—alone.

Chris had met Jonah before, he was sure, but he was having trouble attaching a face to the name. He'd have to go off of Veronica's description.

Taking a deep breath, he put a hand on the door handle. People came in late all the time; it wasn't a big deal to hear the door softly open and the quiet footsteps of families hurrying to their seats. Surely no one would bother turning their heads to see who it was.

He opened the door and scurried through.

What he'd failed to remember was that, while the congregation wasn't facing him, the pastor was. When Pastor Markus paused, his eyes growing wide, the entire population of the church followed suit.

Hundreds of pairs of eyes bored into Chris's. Some portrayed shock, others suspicion, and yet others pity and sadness.

Chris hated it. He loathed every individual stare, no matter the emotion behind it. Hot anger flashed through him.

The pastor continued his sermon almost immediately, flushing apologetically, and Chris ducked his head and shuffled to an empty pew. One by one, the pairs of curious eyes turned back toward the altar.

As the hour dragged on, Chris tried to get a good look around the room for the round-spectacled, vintage clothes-wearing man. However, whenever he glanced up, he'd always find a burning stare looking back at him. The pit in his stomach was growing wider, like a yawning black hole sucking up what was left of his nerve. His fingers clutched the edge of his seat. He could almost see the backs of everyone's heads eroding, two glowing red holes forming in each. All staring. Judging.

He sank deep into his seat and pulled his hood over his head. It was then that he spotted a familiar face. Standing near the front of the room, a tray of communion wafers in hand, was Nick. It was almost as if he was purposely avoiding Chris's eyes. His jaw was tight, his eyes narrowed.

Damnit! I forgot he goes here.

Chris felt like a bird trapped in a cage, a fierce cat prowling just beside him.

The minutes ticked by while the pastor spoke, the clock hand miserably slow.

At last, the pastor gave a closing prayer, a final worship song played, and the congregation was dismissed.

Chris had to stop himself from bolting. His only chance was to go out into the graveyard to see if Jonah was working there. Before he could reach the door, a hand grabbed his arm. His head whipped around, expecting to see Nick towering over him—but no, it was Mr. and Mrs. Ranesh, both of them church elders.

"Christopher, before you go, we were wondering if we could pray for you," said Mr. Rensh softly.

"We know it must have been hard to come today, and we wanted to help you," Mrs. Ranesh whispered with a kind smile.

The tension melted from Chris's shoulders.

"S—sure," he muttered.

With that, they set their hands on his back and prayed for healing. Chris's head felt full of cotton; he barely processed the words they spoke. But soon they were done, and as quickly as they had removed their hands, another set took their place. Then another, and another. Soon several families, though not all, had said their piece to God for Chris. Then they wished him a good day

and told him they hoped he would come back
next week.

Chapter 11
Irises and Willows

The church garden was basically a well-tended backyard. Several stone benches and a stream made it a perfect spot to spend time reading or praying. Beyond a little black wrought-iron gate at the back, the graveyard stretched toward the shaded tree line. Here, the stream became a small river that bordered the burial ground, old weeping willows marking its path.

Underneath one of these willows, a man wearing an embroidered vest and dress pants hummed something from Tchaikovsky as, shovel in hand, he dug a small hole beside a polished tombstone. Apparently satisfied, he straightened his round spectacles before removing an iris from a pot alongside and planting it in the hole. His dirt-brushed hands patted the earth down.

Chris stood just before the waist-high gate.

"Mr. Adamovich?" he called, his eyes forward, avoiding the gravestones.

The man turned to face Chris. He stood slowly and plucked a blue handkerchief from his vest pocket, cleaning his hands on it while he walked over to the gate.

"Greetings!" he called, holding out a hand to Chris, who ignored

it. "Christopher Fara- day, I presume?"

"Yeah. Jonah Adamovich?"

The man nodded. There was a strange warmth about him—like he'd soaked up the sun's rays and displayed them in his smile.

"Are you visiting Mrs. Faraday today? You're welcome to at any time, of course. There aren't any rules regarding that."

Stifling a gulp, Chris shook his head. "I'm here to ask you about the Lady of the Lake."

At this, the man's thick brows rose almost to his hairline. He tucked his kerchief back into its pocket.

"Really, now? Can't say I've been asked about that in a good while! What brought this inquisitive line of thought, eh?"

"Veronica Shores recommended you."

Jonah chuckled. "And she didn't force you to buy a book or fanciful little keyring first?"

"So have you seen the Lady before or not?"

Jonah coughed. "Not in the mood for small talk, I see." He undid the latch of the gate and stepped through. With long, striding steps, he made his way along the garden path and sat on a stone bench beneath a sprawling oak. He motioned toward the wicker chair opposite him. Chris sat down.

Light shone through the round oak leaves and bathed the pair in mottled greens and yellows. Jonah adjusted his glasses and cleared his throat.

"Yes, I've seen her three times; more than anyone else in this town. And I think I've put together a good reason as to why." He steepled his fingers in front of his glasses.

Chris leaned forward.

"The first encounter was when I was but a young boy of around ten. My friends had dared me to climb a particularly steep cliff on Mount Faraday. I had to force myself not to look below, where my friends hollered and teased me while waving their hands. The farther I climbed, the more isolated I felt.

"When I finally reached the cliff's edge and hauled myself up, I could barely hear my friends' cheers over the howling of the wind. I was exhausted—my fingers, I remember, felt like they were going to snap. I looked out onto the expanse of Spectral Lake and Lakes Kelpie and Lullaby beyond. It was perhaps the most breathtaking view I'd ever laid eyes upon. Anyway, after taking a moment to clean my spectacles, I got to my knees and pumped a fist in the air.

"'Take that, Faradays!' I cried, 'I beat your mountain!' Below, my friends hooted. By this time the sun was already dipping low on the horizon.

"That was when I saw a faint flicker on the darkening surface of the lake. Was it an early star reflecting on the water? Well, no. The more I watched, the more the flicker formed into the shape of a woman. She was in a blue dress and floated just above the surface for several minutes before fading into the mist. It was hard to see her clearly, but I was sure I'd spotted the Lady of the Lake. So sure, in fact, that I was too terrified to climb down for hours afterward."

He laughed, the sound rich and warm. "In an event that embarrassed me for months afterward, my friends had to fetch my mother to coax me down. Her strings of Russian admonishments serenaded every step of my descent. I was too ashamed to tell anyone of what I'd seen, but I've kept it with me ever since."

His smile faded, the warmth of nostalgia dimming in his eyes. "The second encounter was just after dusk. I'd been sent to recover the body of a man from the morgue and deliver him to the graveyard. During the journey, my hearse blew a tire and I had to pull over by the lake shore. That was when I got a phone call. It was my wife, Laura, wondering why I wasn't home yet. I explained that the poor man had been hiking on Mount Faraday when he'd contracted a terrible heart attack.

"I finished replacing the tire and opened the hearse to check on the body. The little crucifix I always placed atop caskets when I transported them had fallen off. I took it up in my hands and, as soon as it touched my fingers, I felt a cold chill run down my neck.

"I looked out onto the lake. A green glow beneath the water caught my eye and, before I could even think to step away, a rotting face with pitch-black eyes and wiry hair rose to meet my own. In place of a dress was a lengthy fish-tail, as if the specter were the carcass of a mermaid.

"Well, I held my crucifix before me and uttered terrified prayers. But she didn't appear angry or even vengeful. Only... very sad. Deeply melancholic. She appeared to examine the cross, even brushed her clawed fingers against it—then her gaze turned to me.

"It was the most intense moment I'd ever experienced outside of the Holy Spirit's inner workings. I could hear her breathing, even if no air escaped her nostrils. She looked as if she was trying to recognize me and, when she didn't, she gave a long hiss and sunk beneath the lake once more.

"I never went that route again. Silly, but the experience had a profound effect."

Jonah was quiet for a minute, staring at several doves splashing in a birdbath. With one calloused hand, he rubbed his temple.

"And the third encounter?" Chris murmured.

"Not much of one compared to the last, but still informative, I suppose." He adjusted his vest. "It was when my wife and I were going for a stroll in the evening. Laura decided to wear the silver cross necklace I'd gotten her for our anniversary years ago. It got caught on a branch and the chain broke. The pendant bounced off a rock and fell into the lake water, thankfully only in the shallows on the shore. I bent to pick it up and, when my hands closed around the cross, I saw the Lady's face under the surface. She looked at me only for a moment before sinking back into the depths. I think she recognized me. I asked Laura if she'd seen anything strange, but she hadn't."

Chris nodded slowly, staring into space. Common threads between his own experiences and those of Mr. Adamovich were becoming strikingly apparent.

"The name Faraday and a cross," Chris stated. "Those are the links."

Jonah nodded. "Exactly. Perhaps the Lady is looking for someone from your family. Someone who carried a cross."

"Her husband," Chris said aloud without really having meant to. "Edward Faraday."

Jonah raised an eyebrow. "Really? You think she's a Faraday as well?"

Chris didn't respond.

Jonah cleared his throat. "Mr. Faraday, may I ask why you're interested in this specter? I certainly hope you aren't intent on summoning her. She may not have hurt me, but she may be dangerous if properly provoked. Spiritual matters such as this are intensely... *precarious*."

Chris looked at the doves. They fluffed up their feathers and used their heads to flick drops of water across their little bodies.

Jonah continued. "Even I wouldn't dare do something like that unless I felt God was telling me to do so. Even then..."

Chris watched the smallest of the doves leap into the air as when an oak leaf landed in the water beside it.

"Have you prayed about this, Christopher?"

The dove flew up to the highest branches of the tree. It watched the birdbath carefully and nervously craned its neck up and down.

"Is Christopher bothering you, Mr. Adamovich?"

Chris's posture straightened, his fists clenching.

"Oh, no, not at all, Nicholas," Jonah replied. He rose from his seat. "Though I must admit, Mr. Faraday, that it is getting late. I need to finish my work before the sun dips too low."

Chris nodded. He stood and turned to face

his old friend.

"I think it'd best if you left now, Chris," Nick said. He was standing very still.

Jonah looked at Nick incredulously. "Don't be rude, Nicholas. He can enjoy the garden if he wishes, just like anyone."

"No, it's fine. I'm leaving," Chris said, avoiding Nick's eyes. He nodded at Jonah before setting off for the back door of the church.

He could feel Nick's eyes boring into his back. Somehow, it felt worse than the stares of the congregation.

... After all, Nick was one of those who'd never believed Chris's testimony.

Chapter 12
Reputation

The first thing Chris did when he got back to his apartment was clean and ready his pistol. He hadn't touched it in months. Whether guns had any effect on ghosts or not, he wanted it with him, if only for the confidence boost.

The Lady of the Lake didn't seem violent but, without even knowing her motivations, it was better to be safe than sorry. He wondered whether she could think rationally, whether she could even conceptualize anything beyond what was keeping her tethered to the earth. Chris realized he had no real idea how ghosts worked, and he was loath to trust either the internet or sensationalized local legends.

But, despite all his doubts, the very possibility of contacting his ancestor gave him a secret thrill in the depths of his heart. He hadn't felt *any* sort of motivation or passion for a long time, so finally having something to work for again—a real goal... well, it was *refreshing*.

Chris slid bullets into the magazine before snapping it into place. It was a reassuring weight in his hands, though the slight tremble in his fingers would make aiming difficult. He slipped the gun into the holster strapped to his belt.

The late afternoon sun blazed through the window. It would be hours yet until dusk. Chris paced back and forth around his small living room, stopping to crack open a beer before pacing again.

He glared at the metal cross lying on his desk. There was a small hole drilled in

the top branch, within which was looped a bit of old, frayed rope. Chris cut it away, replacing it with a strong black cord. He took a long drink and tied the cross to his belt.

There was a knock at the door.

Chris froze. Unless his parents were in town, no one ever visited.

He stepped softly toward the door, peeking through the peephole.

It was Esther Quinn.

Chris blinked in surprise. He hadn't seen her for months. She'd never seemed especially interested in him—in fact, he'd barely spoken to her outside of interrogations despite the fact that she'd been assigned to his case. Yet there she stood, arms crossed and face wearing an indeterminable expression. She wasn't in uniform.

Chris tore off his holster and slipped it into a desk drawer. He cracked open the front door.

"Hello?"

"Mr. Faraday?" Esther asked.

"What is it?"

"Just wanted to visit. See how you're doing." Esther shifted her weight from one hip to the other. "Thought you might want some social-ization. Maybe talk with someone."

Chris's brows lowered. "Did Nick put you up to this? What's he trying to choke out of me now?"

Esther shook her head. "No. He just told me he saw you today. Coming here was my idea."

"Why should I believe that?" The anger building in Chris's chest leaked into his voice.

"Listen, we don't have to talk about any-thing you don't want to. You can even rant about that gaming stuff." She absently waved her hand in the air. "I just thought you might want another person to *converse* with is all."

It was still infuriatingly hard to tell what she was thinking. If Chris didn't know better, he might have thought her face was that of a porce-lain doll.

"Why not just email or call or something?"

"If you haven't noticed, I tend to favor the more direct approach."

The air hung empty for a moment. Chris glanced at the cross bumping gently against his leg. His fist closed around the doorknob.

"I don't need help. I'm fine," he said in a low voice.

Esther sighed. "I know. We all think that. But, trust me, it's good to—"

"If you're so concerned, why didn't you do shit to help me when Nick interrogated me five goddamn times?" Chris spat. His voice was betraying a lot more emotion than he'd planned. "And what about when he presented me as a possible suspect, huh? Why didn't you want to 'talk it out' then? Or when he got a search warrant and tore apart my house? My files all combed through like I was a goddamn serial killer?"

There. There it was. A small frown arched across her thin lips.

"Chris, I just—Nick convinced me, okay? I trust him. But lately, I've been feeling like something's just... off about this whole thing. And not in the way he claims."

"All of you put me through hell."

"I know. I want to fix this—to hear your side of the story."

"I've already explained my side *five damn times.*"

"I know, but—"

"You don't believe me. Screw off, Quinn. Take your worthless badge with you."

Chris slammed the door.

No birds were singing. No wind buffeted the surface of the lake or the ducks paddling their way toward breadcrumbs thrown by tourists. A few people strolled the boardwalk or else headed along the beach. Over Faraday Mountain, the sun peeked, as if waiting to see what would happen before it slumbered.

Everything felt eerily still.

The sound of Chris's bike wheels turning and the chain snapping against the metal cogs was meditative, at least. Chris focused on them, trying to ignore the stares of the scarce townspeople. He'd tried to use his sweatshirt to cover the holster, but now he regretted not putting it in a backpack or something.

He rode past a Stop N' Go, then a high school and a bookstore. His path wandered south, back to the place where he'd seen the Lady last.

Nearing Foxglove University, Chris spotted a ramshackle bar down one of the streets to his left. By now, his hands were shaking, so he decided that stopping for a small drink wasn't such a bad idea.

He chained his bike near the entrance and strode in, attempting to hide his face under his hood. While it was worn on the outside, the bar was comparatively well kept within. The floors were swept and bar polished. Sixties classics played softly through a cassette stereo. A few men sat at various tables and several kids who couldn't have been out of their late teens lounged in the very back, their laughter threatening to ruin the bar's serene atmosphere.

Chris's brows furrowed and he glanced back at a shuttered window, looking for any signs ordering patrons to be twenty-one or older. There was one near the door, but it was caked in dust.

Rolling his eyes, Chris sat at the bar and waved at the bartender. She was an older woman, perhaps in her late fifties or early sixties. Her face was lined with wrinkles and her shoulder-length gray hair hung lifelessly around her head. Eyeing Chris sullenly, she removed a cigarette from her lips and rubbed it in a Lullaby Lake-shaped ashtray.

"Fancy seeing you here," she said evenly, her raspy voice betraying her smoking habit as much as the cigarette-filled ashtray. "Saw you in the papers."

"I have a reputation, apparently," Chris said, his finger tapping against the bar. The teenagers had quietened, and were staring at him. One in particular—a redhead decked in punk-looking clothing—was staring at the metal cross with a curious intensity.

"Perhaps. After all, it seems we now have our own little true crime celebrity. Not what our town *wanted* to be known for, I suppose, but with the Lady being our mascot, it seems right to have a ghost-touched fellow as our representative." She wiped her hands on a towel. Her eyes emotionlessly gazed into his.

Chris pulled his hood up higher to block out the teenagers.

"I'd have everyone forget about me if I could," he spat.

"I wouldn't blame you. And I'm sure if you had such an ability, you'd forget about Charlotte as well, wouldn't you?"

Chris's hands to curl into fists.

"What the hell are you talking about?"

"I only mean to say she's caused you quite a bit of pain. She's done that to many of us. Maybe it would have been better for you if you'd never met her at all."

"Y—you piece of shit! What the hell do you know about my life?" Chris rose from his seat. He barely noticed the stares this time.

But the woman said nothing. In fact, she was peering absently at the last trails of smoke drifting from her crushed cigarette. She twisted it in the ashtray, fully smothering the flame. In the low light, she looked tired—sad, even.

"Perhaps she was only using you." The woman's voice cracked. She continued to grind the cigarette against the tray until it crumbled between her fingers. Putting a hand over her mouth, she turned away from Chris.

Fury surging through him, Chris pushed himself away from the bar and flicked the woman his middle finger before bursting out the door. He cursed vehemently under his breath and unchained his bike with shaking fingers.

It was then that the teenagers emerged. The lanky red-headed one stopped before Chris, his hands in the pockets of his leather duster vest.

"Faraday. We were wondering about that cross you've got on," he said in a smooth voice.

"Why?" Chris asked with a sneer.

"It just reminded me of someone I know." The boy blinked slowly. His friends gathered around him. One girl, a studious-looking Latina whose spotless school uniform sat awkwardly alongside the tight shirts and ragged jeans of her punk peers, curled her arm around his and batted her eyelashes. The boy didn't reciprocate her plea for attention. "Tell me where you got it."

Chris narrowed his eyes. Something felt off about this edgy ass-lookin' kid. His eyes were glassy like a marionette's, and his foot twitched impatiently up and down.

"Found it. Thought it would make for a great fashion accessory, like that girl you've got on your arm," Chris snarked.

The boy's face darkened. His friends laughed even as the girl gave them a withering stare.

Chris barreled on. "But, to be honest, I doubt you'd even want this cross. By the look of you, I think you'd burst into flames after touching it."

The boy's companions burst into laughter again. They elbowed the boy and jeered at him.

But the boy's mouth stretched into a thin-lipped smile. He rolled his shoulders back and crossed his arms.

"Say, were you wearing that when you killed Charlotte?" The corners of his mouth twitched upward.

Chris froze.

"Nah, you couldn't have killed her. Don't have the spine. You probably got someone else to do it. Or some*thing*."

Chris's fingernails dug into his palms.

The boy cocked his head to the side. He put a hand under the girl's chin.

"Wonder if the sapphired cross had any-thing to do with it. I hear strange items like that can summon the most curious things. Things that wouldn't leave much evidence."

The boy's friends had stopped laughing and instead looked at the boy with traces of con-fusion. Even the girl looked nervous. "Donovan?" she said.

"So, where did you find it?" His smile was

all teeth now.

Before Chris knew what was happening, his fist was colliding with Donovan's jaw.

The crowd of teens, jeering and shouting, fell into formation. The girl cried out. Donovan stumbled back and hissed between his teeth in pain. It took him a moment to gather himself. His eyes glinted.

"Guess I really hit a nerve, huh? Eye for an eye, nerve for a nerve?" he laughed, his speech slurred.

But Chris barely registered the comment. He was already on his bike and speeding down the street. The teens ran after him at first, but soon gave up. Silently, they watched Chris disappear around the street corner.

Chapter 13
Eleanor

Chris leaned his bike against a tall bush and kicked the nearest tree. He kicked it over and over, streams of curses leaving his mouth with every breath. Finally, he placed his forehead against the trunk and breathed deeply, his arms hanging limply from his shoulders.

The full moon rose overhead, casting a pale light upon the shore. The calls of distant great blue herons mingled with those of crows. Crickets chirped and hopped within thick underbrush.

Chris raised a hand to his face. His knuckles were spotted with blood. He wiped it on the grass, then gazed out at the mirrored surface of the lake.

It was now or never.

He exhaled. The metal cross was cool against his palm. His other hand hovered over his holster.

Step by step, Christopher Faraday made his way to the lake's edge. The wind picked up, whipping around his legs. Finally, he could see his weary face in the water. He looked down at himself for several moments—it had been a while since he'd looked in a mirror.

He'd changed so much since he'd first arrived in this place. Bags hung under his eyes. His SLPD hoodie was worn and fraying in places. His green eyes had lost their shine. His mouth hung in a permanent frown, surrounded by stubble. His hair was uncombed and messy, catching in the breeze.

What's happened to me? Why did I let myself get to this point?

No. It wasn't his fault. It was the world. God. The townspeople.

They did this to me. Not Charlotte.

He ran a hand through his hair and gazed at the metal cross.

If I'm the only one who's gonna solve this shit, then so be it.

And with that, he thrust his cross-toting

hand into the air.

"Eleanor Faraday!" he cried.

The wind howled and screamed. The herons and crows shrieked and launched into the air. The lake rippled and churned.

Chris sucked in breaths when he saw it: a writhing shape beneath the waves.

The festering corpse of a woman slowly rose from the water. Where her legs should have been, a long fishtail curled and slithered, slick with the black liquid that seeped from her mouth. Chris stared. Five bullet holes pierced her chest.

The Lady of the Lake stood just a foot away from Chris, her bony arms tipped with long claws floating at either side of her. She smelled of death. Her black orbs for eyes stared deeply into Chris's own, searching his face. A wet voice escaped her lips.

"Not... Edward..."

Chris struggled to speak. Before he could even reply, the Lady's clawed fingers curled around the cross.

"N—no! I'm not Edward! B—but I am a Faraday! I've come to ask you about Charlotte

Ramsey! I need to know what killed her. Have you seen anything?" Chris was almost hyperventilating now. His body shivered violently.

The Lady wasn't looking at him. Her attention was on the cross.

"*Where is Edward? Oh, where is he? He promised me. James... what has become of James?*" She was muttering more to herself than Chris. Her words little more than quiet sobs. "*James... Edward... is this your cross or mine?*"

The Lady ripped the cross from Chris's fingers and, holding it to her chest, began to slip away, sinking beneath the water. The cross was still strapped to Chris's belt.

"No! *No!*" Chris screamed. She was strong—impossibly strong. He tried to drag himself back to shore but slipped and was brought down to his knees, his body being dragged into the shallows. He pawed at the knot, sputtering water, but his shaking hands skidded over the wet rope. He couldn't see his belt anymore, the water was rising to his chest.

Mind sieged by panic as the dark water overtook him, Chris grasped for his pistol. Coughing, shaking, and blinking away droplets, he took unsteady aim.

A single bullet shot through the water.

The pulling stopped. Chris's head burst out of the lake, his lungs sucking in deep breaths. He dragged himself, choking, back to shore, gun clutched in his dripping hand.

That's when he heard her scream.

The wind threw Chris back into the mud. He rolled in time to see the Lady burst from the water, her face contorted with rage, a fresh hole pierced through her tail.

"*Evil, evil Edward! Sent a boy to shoot me?*" she crowed.

Then she was upon him, her claws digging into his shoulders. Ice shot through Chris's veins as he cried out.

"*Why? Why! He said he would come back!*" the Lady wailed. "*Set me free!*"

Chris writhed under her grip. His arms were numb, immobile—his blood frozen.

"Let me go!" Chris cried. "I'm not Edward! I don't know him! I'm Chris! Chris Faraday! Aaa—*Ah!*" The claws dug deeper, blood beginning to soak through his jacket.

The Lady pressed her face into his. Pitch-black hollows scanned his face, her mouth curled into a dreadful frown.

"*James?*" She gasped. "*James! You've come back! I—I—*"

In one swift motion, the Lady jerked away. She was trembling. Her body seemed to morph and stretch, her skin cracking and arms making sickening popping sounds. She was crying softly, even as her body broke.

"*Where have I been? What have I been doing? I... Oh...*" Her eyes closed, and a low, mournful sigh escaped her lips.

The green, rotting skin peeled away, as did the fishtail. Beneath, a beautiful woman in an elegant draping dress emerged, hands clasped to her chest. She glowed a faint blue, and her translucent body let through the light of the moon. A ghostly cross—identical to the one hanging from Chris's belt—dangled from her neck.

She opened her eyes. They were no longer black, but clear and white, with striking blue pupils. They swiveled, widening, as if seeing for the first time. The woman took in the scene with quiet sophistication, though her shoulders sagged when she saw Chris.

"What have I done?" she whispered. Tears sparkling like little diamonds slid down her cheeks.

Chris could barely move. His whole body felt numb—paralyzed, and he stared at the Lady like a bird in a trap. Fresh blood dripped from his shoulders and down his neck.

"James... I'm so sorry..." the Lady said. "I never—I didn't think I'd ever become a polter- geist. I—I just wasn't strong enough."

Chris's mouth was dry. He

didn't know what to say.

The Lady's head cocked to one side. Her hands pressed against her chest.

"It's been so long since I've seen you, little one." Her voice choked up. "You've grown so much!"

She glanced at the blood. "Oh, goodness, I apologize. I don't know what came over me. I've seen this happen to others so many times, and yet I never thought it would happen to me—I couldn't fathom what it would be like to feel myself so reduced." Her voice softened. "James, I'm sorry you had to see me like that."

She kneeled beside him. Her delicate gloved fingers gently pulled down the collar of the hoodie so she could get a better look at the wounds.

"They aren't terribly deep, thankfully." She sighed. "I must admit that your clothes are dreadfully strange." She examined his jeans. "Have you been working in the mines?"

Chris didn't answer. His voice was just coming back to him.

"Has the cat got your tongue? Did I frighten you that badly?" She bit her lip. "Don't worry, you'll be able to move again soon."

Indeed, warmth was already returning to his limbs. He coughed violently before taking a shaking breath.

"Are you... Eleanor Faraday?" he asked wearily.

She nodded, frowning. "Don't you recognize me? Didn't your father ask you to come here?"

Chris winced. "I... I'm not James. I'm Christopher. Your great-great-grandson."

Eleanor's eyes were unfocused. Her hands moved to cover her mouth.

"It's been that long...?"

She drifted upward as if taken by a stray gust and turned away from Chris. In the distance, the town glowed, electric lights and neon signs obscuring the stars overhead. Car headlights raced past buildings before disappearing.

"No..."

She buried her head in her hands.

"They left me. They never came back."

A poisonous green was snaking up Eleanor's dress. Grunting, Chris lunged, grasping the hem of her skirt.

"Stay with me, Eleanor," he said, his heart thundering even as his hand froze.

Eleanor gazed back at him, the light blue once again overtaking the green.

"Of course, of course, I can't get overwhelmed again." She rubbed her eyes. "Thank you."

It was as if she was looking at him anew; like he was an entirely new person.

"Christopher..." she murmured, as if trying the name on her lips. "It's a pleasure to meet you." She reached down to shake his hand. He very reluctantly obliged, then climbed slowly to his feet.

"I've been looking for you," he sputtered.

"I see. I assume Edward passed down my story—though I have no idea why it's taken so long for someone to come for me." Eleanor shook her head. "No wonder I was a poltergeist."

Chris gulped. "Eleanor, I'm afraid it wasn't Edward's doing." He paused. "I never heard that you needed to be found. The reason I'm here is *different.*"

Eleanor straightened. "What?"

"My family never passed down stories about you. I didn't even know your name until I found this cross on the lakeside. The Faradays... Edward moved to Texas and went back to horse ranching after you died. We never knew why." Chris swallowed. "It's a miracle I even discovered that you were related to me."

Eleanor didn't respond.

"Did he... Did he kill you? Is that why you live in the lake?" Chris took a cautious step back.

Her cheeks blanched white. "Yes. But it wasn't like it sounds. It wasn't like that at all."

Chris turned his head expectantly.

"If he hadn't shot me, I would have killed him and my son, James." Her eyes were downcast. "I was possessed."

A heron's call echoed in the night. A raven responded in kind.

"He shot me, and I fell into the lake. The poltergeist that possessed me dragged me down into the depths. I took my last breath and awoke anew." One of her fingers hovered above a gunshot wound in her chest. Chris could see through it to the lake beyond. "He called to me and said he would come back. He wept as he ushered our son away from the scene. He said he would exorcize me from this world so I could be free to return to my maker."

The heron called again. This time, the raven did not answer.

"Was he a pastor? Could he even do that?"

Eleanor raised her head in surprise. "Well, yes, but, more importantly, he was a Faraday. It's what we do."

"I'm not following."

Eleanor blinked slowly. "We're paranormal investigators. We've always been."

"What?"

"Please don't tell me you've never known!" Eleanor cried. She pointed to the cross at Chris's leg. "The cross with three sapphires; that is our badge. It is how people recognized our profession. The metal is a tool; it frosts over when near a ghost."

Chris looked down. Indeed, the cross was layered with fine white frost.

"We were both missionaries and exorcists. We guided lost souls snagged on the coils of this mortal realm to the afterlife. I cannot believe Edward and James never passed this down! It is our legacy—not just of the Faradays, but also of my maiden name!"

"You can't be serious."

"Well, you can see me, can you not? Not everyone can so easily observe a spirit."

Chris rubbed his forehead. "I thought we were horse ranchers. Wasn't that our legacy?"

"Well, yes. But that was mostly the duty of the eldest son. The other children were trained to help with the ranch, but also in the... *lesser-known* trade of the family. Edward broke tradition by focusing entirely on the paranormal despite being the eldest. But, to be perfectly frank, that was due to my own influence."

Eleanor hesitated. The wind had picked up again. Dark, broiling clouds moved to block out the moon. A drizzle of rain began.

Multiple pieces of a great puzzle were coming together in Chris's mind. Eleanor's words were confusing and ludicrous and yet crystal-clear. Chris stepped back, suddenly acutely aware of a throbbing headache.

"Perhaps we should head to your home. You are likely to catch a terrible cold in this weather, besides the fact that you're sopping wet. And those wounds need to be treated." Eleanor nodded matter-of-factly.

"Wait, *we*?"

"Well, it appears my husband and son never passed down our work to the next generation. I would be loath to leave this earth without training at least one successor." She crossed her arms, an expression of solemn determination on her face.

"No. No! I came to find you for one reason and one reason only." Chris took a deep breath, collecting his scattered thoughts and wincing as Charlotte's face appeared in his mind.

"My—my wife. Charlotte. She was"—

Chris pulled his eyes away from the tarp-covered memorial—"killed. By *something*. A ghost, a monster, I don't goddamn know." He wiped his eyes.

Eleanor's expression softened.

"I just—I need you to tell me if you saw anything, or if you know what that monster is." Chris stuck his hands in his pockets.

"What do you plan on doing with that monster when you find it?" Eleanor asked quietly.

"I'll kill it," Chris spat. "I'll do whatever it takes to get rid of it forever."

"You won't be able to do that without my help."

Chris's eyes darted up to Eleanor's. "So you've heard of it? What do you know?"

"I know that whatever it is, you won't be able to exorcise it. Not without training."

"I dealt with you, didn't I?"

Eleanor's mouth twisted into a frown. "The only thing that saved you from me was your face, Christopher. If I hadn't seen the family resemblance... well, I don't want to even think about what could have happened. You're lucky, not talented."

"I don't need your help. Just tell me what it is and where it is." Chris's face darkened.

"What did it look like?"

"A large, black... shadow. It had an ax and bright red holes in its head."

Eleanor's face blanched. "Oh. Oh no, Christopher. You can't take that on. Not now."

"Why?"

"Just let me train you. You need me."

Chris's face contorted. "No, I don't. I can do it on my own! Tell me where it is!"

"I won't leave until you let me."

"No!"

Eleanor rose above him, her tone ascending to a yell. "Christopher, "you don't understand! I *can't* leave this earth unless I help you! The last two things tethering me to this world are the fact that none of my descendants are fulfilling the legacy I left behind, despite the promises of my husband and son. That, and neither of them ever came back for me!" Her voice broke. "And if you get yourself killed by wandering into a powerful poltergeist you hardly even understand, I could never forgive myself! Both you and I would likely be trapped in this accursed prison of a lake forever! Would Charlotte want that?"

The air fell still. Fat drops of rain splashed against the memorial tarp. The smell of wet grass and pine needles wafted between slick trunks.

Chris turned away from Eleanor and walked back toward his bike.

"Maybe she does."

He mounted the bike and rode off down the muddy path. Eleanor watched him leave, wind whistling through the bullet holes puncturing her wispy frame.

Chapter 14
Lost Echoes

Chris barely slept that night. He was exhausted and still sore, even after the painkillers. Groaning, he got up out of bed, filled the sink, and tried to scrub the bloodstains out of his shirt and hoodie. It was slow going.

Heavy bouts of rain rolled down the windows. Over the sink, a single light bulb bathed the room in a dull glow. Low synth music played in Chris's headphones.

It was three in the morning—the hour when everything felt dead.

Chris's hands were swollen with moisture. The sink ran, draining water taking with it the bloody smears Eleanor had left behind. He scrubbed a sponge against his jacket over and over in the same pattern, as if lost in a trance.

"Christopher..." a muffled voice called, piercing through his headphones and caressing

Chris's ears.

Chris started, dropping the sponge and jacket.

"Christopher..."

It was a woman's voice, but not Eleanor's. It came from the closet.

Chris gently lifted his pistol from the desk. He turned slowly toward the closet, his shaking hand reaching for the knob.

He turned it, and the door gradually swung open. The closet was full of tightly wrapped cardboard boxes. One, however, was open, its contents spilled on the carpet. Picture frames wrapped in newspaper peeked out under packing peanuts.

Chris hesitated. Sweat beaded on his forehead. From beneath a wrapped frame, muffled music rose, a voice softly singing along.

Gently, Chris got to his knees and took the frame in his hands. He unwrapped it.

The picture was of him and Charlotte on a boat at the lake. It seemed to move and swim, like a video playing on a screen. The water rippled, trees swayed, and Chris's hands strummed gently on the blue ukulele. Charlotte's lips moved, her head in his lap.

Chris stared at the frame for a long time. It was as if he could feel the warmth emanating from her voice.

For the first time in a very long while, Chris let himself cry.

"*Don't leave me, Christopher.*"

"I won't."

"*It's coming for me.*"

"I'll protect you."

"*I can't leave this place. I need you to stay with me.*"

"I will. Always."

"*It's coming, Christopher. It's coming!*"

Black shadows slithered along the walls. They pulsated and seeped between the boxes. Red holes burned within every surface, as if the walls were spotted with windows for demons to spy through.

The shadows grew larger, grasping at Chris. He didn't notice. His eyes were fixed on the picture.

"*It's cold and dark and alone.*"

"I know."

"*I can't breathe.*"

The shadows crept up his neck.

"Where are you?"

There was only a pained shriek in reply. Chris jerked suddenly, noticing with a start the shadows crawling into his mouth and down his throat. He leaped up, limbs flailing, fingers digging and ripping at nothing. His screams bubbled up from lungs filling with black water. He reached for his gun and swung it toward his head.

His finger twitched on the trigger.

A blue streak of light hit him from his side. The gun was knocked from his hand and skittered across the floor.

"Leave him at once!" a voice commanded. "Be gone in the name of the Lord!"

In the presence of the light, the shadows fled, their slimy tails disappearing into the darkest corners of the room. Chris collapsed on the floor, retching up water and blood. A cool hand grasped Chris's own.

"Listen to me. Follow my voice," Eleanor's gentle words ordered.

"I heard Charlotte... I need to find her. She... needs me," Chris said between coughs, his thoughts laced with delirium.

"You will. But the shadows will overtake you if you refuse to obtain the knowledge needed to combat them. Don't you see that now?"

Chris's head lolled onto its side. "How are you here?"

"I followed you."

Chris nodded slowly, staring at the floor.

"And it's just as well I did. You could clearly use the help." Eleanor's voice dropped. "And so could I, really."

Rubbing his bloodshot eyes from the remnants of derangement, Chris rose into a sitting position and stared at Eleanor. His mind warred with itself, but he was too damn tired to properly brood over this. He had to make a decision.

"What do you say, great-great-grandson?" Eleanor held out a gloved hand. "Are you prepared to engage in the wonders of untangling unfortunate spirits from their earthly tethers?"

Chris let out a long sigh. The horrors he'd been through had shaken him to the core and, although he found outside interference and piteous sympathy distasteful in the extreme, there was something else there too; a new feeling rising in his chest. *Comfort*.

"Fine. What the hell." He grasped Eleanor's hand in his and shook it.

"Thank you, Christopher." Despite the frigid touch of her grasp, Eleanor's smile was as warm as the morning sun that was beginning to eke through the window.

An elegant gradient of blue to golden orange stretched across a tree-filled sky; the sky whose light reflected in the deep, deep waters of Spectral Lake.

End of Book 1

Concept Art

Here are a few bits of concept art I created over the years for Spectral Lakes, even before knowing it was going to be a book!

InkRose

187

Promotional Artwork for the Spectral
Lakes Animation KickStarter

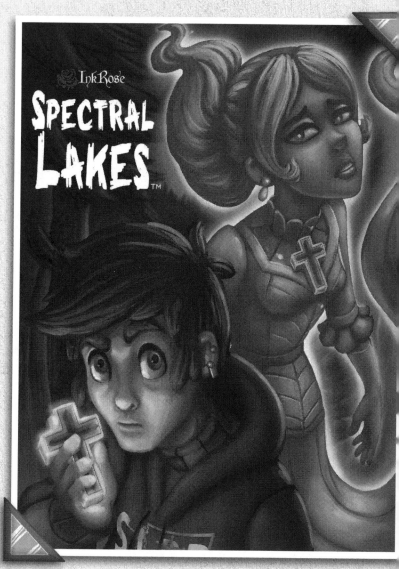

Esther and Nick First Concepts

First-ever iterations of Charlotte and
Chris, made in 2017.

193

About Ink Rose

Hey there, I'm just a girl who really likes writing and drawing cool characters. When I grew up I always wanted to be a fairy-mermaid. Unfortunately I'm just a YouTuber/Artist now. Bit of a downgrade, but I have a lot of fun with what I do. Getting to make people cry is great.

I'm always looking to improve my craft. Hopefully I'll be able to reach the "ArtStation Legend" status at some point in the future.
Thanks for taking the time to bear with my wonky anatomy and long-winded character descriptions.

Anyway, I suppose you could always check out more of my art n' stuff on my website. I also really like to attend conventions. Selling my book to people face-to-face beats working retail.

And yes, despite how I look, I can assure you I am over 21 years old.

InkRoseInc.com